Cl ra braced her arms against the table in front
of he On the next thrust Clara felt Belinda's hand
slide side. Clara cried out as intense pleasure shot
thro h her. She pushed back onto the hand that
Beli a gently thrust into her. Clara's muscles
clam d around Belinda's hand, trying to keep it
insid her. Belinda was talking to her, but Clara
coul t hear her over the roar of her own rushing
bloo Clara's body tensed only seconds before she
cam so hard she felt wetness running down her
thigh

RHYTHM TIDE

Frankie J. Jones

THE NAIAD PRESS, INC.
1998

Printed in the United States of America on acid-free paper
First Edition

Editor: Lila Empson
Cover designer: Bonnie Liss (Phoenix Graphics)
Typesetter: Sandi Stancil

Library of Congress Cataloging-in-Publication Data

Jones, Frankie J., 1953–
    Rhythm tide / by Frankie J. Jones
        p.   cm.
    ISBN 1-56280-189-9 (pbk.)
    I. Title.
PS3560.04825R48   1997
813'.54—dc21   97-40376
                                                                        CIP

To Peggy
For putting laughter in my heart

Acknowledgments

I would like to thank my Mama, who taught me persistence, and Martha Cabrera, for reading the manuscript and lending her words of wisdom. And Peggy J. Herring, for always being there.

About the Author

Frankie J. Jones grew up between the soybean rows and cotton stalks of Southeast Missouri, better known to its inhabitants as the Bootheel. While in the Army she met her life partner, Peggy J. Herring. They currently live in South Texas as far away from cotton stalks as Frankie can get. When not working at her eight-to-five job or writing, Frankie spends her time working in the bookstore she and Peggy own. When she finds a free moment she likes to spend it reading, metal detecting, or researching the numerous shipwrecks off the Texas coast.

CHAPTER ONE

The cold damp of the rock crept deep into Clara's bones as she sat hypnotized by the crashing waves. The swirling water hissed, fighting to break free of gravity's pull, only to be sucked back into the Gulf. Relentless April wind worried the tight knot of hair at the nape of her neck until the beaten strands slowly surrendered. Not even the lonesome cry of the gulls penetrated the vacuum of her emotions.

It would be so easy, she thought. *Just stand up and walk until my feet no longer touch bottom and swim until my arms refuse to carry me. And then at long last there would be peace.*

The voices of the water sirens were calling her, and she was too emotionally drained to resist them. Two steps out and the murky foam swirled around her ankles. Allen would be angry when he discovered her note, but he would be angrier that she had taken the car.

With a twinge of guilt, she realized she was ruining her best shoes, delicate tan suede heels with deep chocolate insets. In an act totally alien to her nature, she had bought them knowing that Allen would be upset by her extravagance. He was always upset at her about something. She kicked off the heels and felt the soft sand sink under her feet.

The hem of her skirt grew wet as she continued to walk. Why had she worn her best suit? She loved its deep-cream color, the jacket severely closed with tiny pearl buttons. It was a shame to ruin it. Someone else could have used it. Slowly she released the pearl buttons, removed the jacket, and let it drop.

The water swirled around her waist. Walking against its constant pressure was difficult, but she pushed on. She had to walk as far as possible to save her arms for that last long swim. Her body must not be brought back in by the tide. She wanted to rest forever, hidden from . . . from what? Allen, the boys, or just the world in general? A world in which she was no longer able to cope. A world that had excluded her from its secrets of survival. A wave licked her neck like the gentle tease of a lover.

When her feet no longer touched bottom, she began to swim in short, choppy strokes. Swimming was one more thing she was terrible at. Allen and the boys were so graceful. Jamie had been a much better swimmer than she was when he was only three, but Jamie was just like his father.

Chubby, freckled cheeks and clinging, pudgy hands reached for her and pulled her farther from the shoreline. These were the images of her sons that she chose to remember, not those of the rapidly maturing young men who grew more distant from her each day.

Would they grow up to be just like their father? No! She slapped at the water harshly. Her sons would not be like Allen. Hadn't she instilled enough of her own values in them to prevent that? But Jamie, her older son, was already a developing carbon copy of Allen. Roger's temperament was more like her own. What would happen to him now that she was no longer there? Her arms ached, and a heaviness settled over her body. She forced herself to push on until her arms could no longer support her.

Closing her eyes, she surrendered to the gentle tugging that pulled her beneath the surface. Her chest tightened as her body consumed the last molecules of oxygen. For a moment, instinct made her body fight the pull of the water, but she forced herself to relax until the soft tranquillity of freedom cradled her.

Her newfound peace was shattered when an arm slid around her waist, yanking her upward. She screamed in pain as her head emerged from the water and oxygen filled her empty lungs. Salt water burned her eyes. *No!* her brain shouted, fighting to return to the watery solitude.

A hand closed around her collar and held her head above water. "You have no right!" she screamed

3

as anger shot adrenaline through her body. "You can't stop me!" She plunged forward and tried to swim away from the intruder, but the grasp was too firm. Changing tactics, she threw her head backward, which caused a blinding pain to rip through her skull as it struck against the stranger's head. There was a soft grunt. The hand slipped from her collar, leaving only the arm around her waist. Clara tried to fling it off. Her struggling forced them deeper into the water, but the arm refused to be shaken loose. Again a sense of peace descended over her. Clara smiled. This time she had won. With a silent good-bye to Jamie and Roger, she closed her eyes and made one last feeble attempt to shake free of the arm still entangled around her. Softly she settled upon a clump of seaweed. As the intruder's body nestled against hers, Clara's inner alarm sounded: She wasn't drowning alone. This was not what she had wanted.

Panic propelled her. Grabbing the stranger's arm, she battled her way upward, her own urgent need for air pushing her harder. An eternity passed before her head shot above the water and oxygen again tore into her lungs, paralyzing her with a fit of coughing. A wave slapped against her face, and she automatically swallowed to keep from choking. The salt water gagged her. She forced the limp body over onto its back. The woman's pale face and blue-tinted lips told her she had no time to waste.

Clara struggled toward the shore, cursing herself for allowing her own weakness and stupidity to harm someone else, and cursing the woman for interfering. She struggled against the pull of the outgoing tide. The same water that had only moments before offered her a peaceful haven was now ugly and demanding. It wasn't willing to give her up. It fought and grabbed at her, determined to retain its hold.

A strangled shout of joy escaped her aching throat when she felt the sandy bottom brush against her feet. Digging into the sand, she pushed forward until at last she was able to drag the limp body to shore.

Ignoring the burning ache rushing through her arms, Clara fought to recall the lifesaving drills she had helped Jamie and Roger practice. What had *The Official Boy Scout Handbook* said? Pinch the nose? No, clear the mouth first. Now tilt the chin and pinch the nose ... blow.

"Please breathe," she begged while trying to blow life into the woman. Clara shivered violently as a cool wind blew through her wet clothing.

At last, the woman groaned, coughed heavily, and rolled onto her side, spewing salt water into the sand. As more choking coughs tore from her, Clara slumped back, her body shaking with exhaustion.

The woman rolled onto her back, gasping for air. Soft gray eyes focused on Clara, and comprehension slowly returned. Her eyes grew dark with anger. "You damn fool." She struggled to sit up and began coughing again. Catching her breath, she continued. "You almost killed us both." She stopped to breathe. "What the hell were you doing out there? Can't you read?" She pointed to a large red-and-white *No Swimming* sign that in truth Clara hadn't noticed.

The woman's anger sparked Clara's own. Why did everyone feel they had a right to tell her what to do? "I wasn't swimming. It's none of your business." Anger and her aching throat choked off the words. "If you'd left me alone it would've all been over by now." Springing to her feet, she ran toward the water. The woman shot forward and threw her arms around Clara's legs, toppling them into the sand. Clara kicked savagely, but the woman's grasp held firm. Closing her eyes against the tears, Clara welcomed the sting of the sand as it ground into her flesh. Too exhausted to care any longer, she stopped struggling and lay facedown, sobbing.

"It can't be that bad," the woman said finally, still clinging to Clara's legs.

"How do you know?"

"It can't be worth killing yourself over." She released Clara and sat up with her back to the water. Her anger seemed to have vanished as suddenly as it had appeared.

Clara started to rise, and the woman leaned toward her. Clara moved slowly and sat up. While wiping sand and tears from her face, she studied the sharp thin features that were framed in a mop of short, black hair that the water had plastered into odd shapes around the woman's almost handsome face. Under a layer of wet sand, she was wearing a pale blue sweatshirt, black shorts, and one sneaker. Her toes on the bare foot were slowly burrowing into the sand. This woman had saved her life.

A savage chill ripped through Clara's body, causing her to shake uncontrollably. Her teeth began to snap together so harshly she feared they'd shatter. She had almost killed them both. Allen was right — she was crazy.

The woman was beside her talking. Clara gazed into her soft gray eyes and tried to concentrate on what she was saying. But she was suddenly too tired, and she surrendered to the exhaustion.

CHAPTER TWO

Clara slowly woke to the sound of a crackling fire and the smell of fresh coffee. For the briefest moment, the sounds and smells produced a profound sense of peace for her. She could feel the warm flannel sheets caressing her skin and smell the vague scent of strawberries clinging to the soft downy pillow. She had the odd sense of being a child again and being at her grandmother's. The spell shattered as the memories flooded back. The peace she had been searching for was gone again. Blinking the room into focus, she found herself lying in a massive four-poster bed. Across from the bed, a curtainless bay window displayed gray dismal clouds. An empty easel loomed in front of the window, its skeletal frame stark against the sky. The woman sat on a chocolate brown couch, staring into the flames. Clara moved slightly, and she looked up.

Smiling, she rose from the couch and approached the bed. She was wearing a short, yellow terry-cloth robe. Seeing the pale purple bruise above the woman's left eye, Clara blushed as she remembered striking back with her head while trying to free herself from the woman's grip.

"How are you feeling?"

Unable to meet the clear gray eyes, Clara focused on the fire. No wonder Allen had gone to other women. Why would he want to come home to someone as crazy as she was? Her raw throat burned as she swallowed tears.

"Here. Sit up." The woman stuffed an extra pillow behind her. Crossing the room to the stove, she returned with a steaming mug of soup. "Try some of this. It'll make you feel better."

Clara glanced at the cup and covered her face with her hands. Never had she been so ashamed.

There was a scraping sound as the woman set the soup down before gathering Clara into her arms. "It's okay."

Clara tried to pull away, but the embrace was firm and offered a sense of security. She gave in and let her tears seep into the warmth of the robe, which also smelled faintly of strawberries.

* * * * *

When she woke again, rain was beating against the window. The woman stood with her head resting on the glass, staring out. She had changed into a red sweater and jeans. As if feeling Clara's eyes on her, she turned around.

"I'm sorry." Clara's words came out a raw croak.

"Forget it. It's over with." She took a pack of cigarettes from her shirt pocket and offered the pack to Clara, who declined. Lighting one for herself, she turned back to the window.

Clara used the time to study her surroundings more closely. It was a large open area that was divided into a kitchen, a living room, and a bedroom, simply by its arrangement. The utilitarian kitchen was only a few feet from the end of the bed. To her right, a splash of color radiated from the bright multihued patchwork quilt that was thrown over the back of the couch. Across from the couch and next to the fireplace was a round wooden table that held a tiny portable television. The walls and floors were smooth weathered wood, with no sign of paint. While nothing seemed to actually match, there was a sense of warmth that Clara found comforting. It was the complete opposite of her own precisely decorated home that she had once been so proud of.

The woman slowly ground the cigarette out in an oyster-shell ashtray. "There's fresh coffee, and I was about to make some lunch. Why don't you join me?"

Clara shook her head.

"You should eat. It'll make you feel better."

"I ate this morning," Clara croaked, watching her move about the tiny kitchen. Actually she couldn't remember the last time she had eaten, but the thought of food repelled her.

"You've been here since yesterday."

"Yesterday!" Clara sat up sharply. The sudden movement caused the room to spin. She leaned back and tried to remember when she had left. Monday. "What day is this?"

The woman stopped taking down dishes and stared at her. "Thursday."

Clara closed her eyes to think. She had been gone for four days. After leaving Shreveport she had driven at random, and most of her time on the road was a blur. She remembered stopping for gas a few times and falling asleep at a roadside park. What were Allen and the boys doing? Were they worried about her?

As if reading her thoughts, the woman pointed. "There's a phone by the bed if you need to call someone." She busied herself pulling pans from under the cabinet.

"No. No one."

"There must be somebody worrying about you."

Clara looked up to find her staring again. The woman's gaze traveled to the pale circle left by the wide wedding band Clara had worn for almost twenty years. Guiltily, Clara stuck her hands under the blanket to hide the telltale mark.

"No," Clara replied and pushed herself into a more comfortable position in the bed.

Shrugging, the woman turned to the refrigerator and pulled out a plastic bowl, a jar of mayonnaise, and packages of luncheon meat. "By the way, my name's Randi Kosub."

"Randy."

"Yeah, Randi with an *i*." From the bowl she dumped cold soup into a pan. "My father wanted a boy."

"Was he terribly disappointed?" Clara remembered how much she had wanted her second child to be a girl.

"A little, but he changed his mind." She glanced at Clara. "I suppose you have a name?"

"Clara." She decided to omit the last name.

"Well, Clara, I'm going to have a sandwich and some soup. It'll be ready in about ten minutes if you'd like to join me."

Clara sat, not wanting to move, but the smell of the soup and her grumbling stomach finally convinced her to move. Throwing back the blanket, she found she was dressed in an unfamiliar blue-flannel shirt. Her face burned with embarrassment at the thought of this woman undressing her. During one of their many fights after Roger was born, Allen had told her that her body was disgusting to look at. Since then she had taken great pains to hide it.

"I drove you up in your car. I didn't want to dig through your stuff, so I put one of my shirts on you. I'm afraid the clothes you were wearing are ruined." Randi paused while slicing an onion. "Your purse and suitcase are in the bathroom. It's on the right," she said, nodding toward an area Clara had been unable to see from the bed.

Clara pulled the shirt down as far as possible and walked quickly into the narrow hallway. There were two doors on the left side, both of which were closed. Shutting the bathroom door, she leaned against it unsteadily. The simplicity of the room's almost nonexistent decor soothed her. A long closet ran down

11

one side of the room; her suitcase and purse sat by it. The walls and floor were of the same unstained wood as the main room. A large red-and-yellow rag rug covered most of the floor. The walls were bare except for two small, unframed seascapes and an old-fashioned wooden medicine cabinet with a mirror.

Her pale reflection was a shock, and seeing it brought back yesterday's events full force. If Randi had not intervened, she would have been dead now. Her lungs seemed suddenly to collapse. Unable to inhale enough air to satisfy them, she slid to the floor and rested her head against her knees. As she fought to regain control, chills ripped through her.

Stripping off the shirt, she crawled into the shower and turned on the hot water. Steam was soon bellowing out, but the water still felt cold to her. Even after her skin turned deep red, she continued to stand in the near-scalding water until the shaking stopped and her breathing returned to normal. Stepping out of the shower, she rapidly dried herself.

After a quick survey of the contents of her suitcase, she slipped on a navy-blue skirt and a white blouse. She carefully arranged her wet hair into the tight knot she had worn for the past twelve years. Allen liked her hair long, but it was constantly in her way and she preferred to wear it up. As she applied her makeup, she forced herself to examine her face closely. At forty-one there were dark circles under her eyes. Without its regular brown rinse, her naturally curly hair would be heavily streaked with gray. The wrinkles in the corner of her brown eyes were deeper than she remembered. With one last pat of her hair, she took a deep breath and returned to the kitchen.

Except for the rain that pounded against the bay window, they ate in silence. Afterward, Randi poured them coffee and suggested they move to the couch. Clara watched Randi place a log on the fire to chase away the damp chill. The flames shot up bright and warm.

Randi lit a cigarette and once more extended the pack. Clara started to decline, but hesitated as the enticing smell of the freshly lit cigarette reached her. She had smoked until she had met Allen, but he hadn't liked the smell and she quit. Seeing her hesitate, Randi lit another one and handed it to her. Clara held it, watching the smoke curl up and away. Allen's angry eyes seemed to glare at her from the glowing ash. In defiance, she lifted the cigarette and took a long drag. The hot smoke seared her raw throat and lungs. She coughed harshly and fought to catch her breath. She glanced at Randi, expecting to see her laughing at her childishness, but she seemed to be deeply engrossed in the flickering fire.

Clara wiped the tears from her eyes. What do you say to a person you almost killed? She cleared her throat and nervously shifted. "I'm really sorry about yesterday. I hope you're all right." She pointed to the bruise over Randi's eye.

"I'm fine," Randi reassured her, placing the oyster-shell ashtray between them. "It's a small bruise."

Clara looked at a clock on the fireplace mantel. It was almost five. She stood and tugged at a loose strand of hair. "I should be going."

"The weather's getting worse. You're welcome to spend the night if you'd like."

Clara eyed the rain with some trepidation. She

had no idea where she would go, but she had already caused Randi enough trouble. "I really should be going." She walked to the window and was startled to see palm trees and an endless stretch of water. "Where am I?"

Randi raised an eyebrow. "Just outside of Rockport." At Clara's blank stare she added, "You're about forty-five miles from Corpus Christi."

"Texas!"

Randi shrugged and grinned before replying, "The last time they surveyed, it was."

Clara searched her memory. She couldn't remember crossing the state line. Her knees went weak. Would Allen report his car stolen? Could a husband charge his wife with car theft?

"Care to talk about it?"

"What?" Clara asked, startled.

"Suit yourself, but I really don't think you should leave tonight. It's getting nasty out there." At Clara's hesitation, she added, "Look, if you want, you can stay for a few days. Not many people are around this time of year." She shrugged. "Of course, if you decide to stay you have to sleep on the couch."

Clara looked up to see her smiling, and she quietly considered her options. She had no idea where she was going or what she would do once she got there. If she stayed here for a day or two it would give her time to make some sort of plan. She looked sideways at the woman who had opened up her home to her. Why was she living way out here alone? Clara judged her to be close to her own age. Was she married? She glanced at Randi's hands. There was no wedding band. Why was this stranger helping her?

14

Whatever her reasons were, Clara realized she was extremely grateful.

"Thank you," Clara said, returning to the couch and sitting down. *Tomorrow I'll make a decision*, she promised herself.

"I have to drive to Corpus in the morning," Randi said. "You're welcome to come along if you want."

"I think I'll stay here and rest, if you don't mind."

"Sure. Let me know if you change your mind." Getting up, Randi switched on the television and settled quietly on her end of the couch. They spent the remainder of the evening watching the television in silence.

CHAPTER THREE

Clara woke early, as usual. Without thinking, she rolled out of bed and reached for her robe. It wasn't on the chair where it had been every morning for almost two decades. Memories of the past few days flooded back as she slowly sat on the couch.

Allen and the boys weren't here. There'd be no one to fix breakfast for. No laundry, cleaning, or shopping to do. No errands to run. How did single people spend their days? *They work,* she told herself, heading into the bathroom where she quickly dressed and put her hair up.

Returning to the kitchen, she made coffee and sat quietly at the table. The room began to fill with the aroma of the perking brew.

Randi sat up in bed suddenly, clutching the quilt to her.

"I'm sorry if I woke you," Clara mumbled hastily.

"No, I need to get up." She sat blinking. "I've got a lot to do today." She pulled the yellow robe off the bedpost and slipped into it.

Clara was embarrassed to see that Randi slept nude. She hid her discomfort by getting up and pouring them coffee.

"If you like I could fix breakfast," she offered as Randi sat down at the table.

"Not for me. If I get hungry I'll pick something up on the way in. Why don't you change your mind and go with me?"

Clara shook her head. "I'd better not."

Randi sipped her coffee. "You're a long way from Louisiana," she replied evenly, staring into her cup.

Startled, Clara's hand jerked, causing her coffee to spill. "How did you know I'm from Louisiana?" She got a paper towel to clean up the mess.

"The license plate on your car."

Silence hung between them, and Clara suddenly felt trapped.

"Look," Randi said, "it's none of my business, but I'd like to help if I can. Sometimes things aren't so bad if you talk about them."

Clara shredded the soggy paper towel and felt like a fool. What could she say? I'm forty-one and I ran away from home. Decent mothers don't run off and leave their children! Jamie and Roger had been her reason for living for so long, but during the last two or three years they seemed to decide they no longer needed her for anything other than maid service. Now she felt lost and confused about her role in their lives. She needed time to sort things out. Realizing that Randi was waiting for an answer, she shook her head. "Not yet."

"The offer stands if you change your mind." Randi drained her coffee cup and left the room. When she returned she was dressed in a dark green sweatshirt, jeans, and a pair of sneakers, her hair still wet from the shower. Going to the door, Randi removed a ring of keys from a nail driven into the frame. "You're sure you don't want to go?"

"No, thanks."

Randi leaned against the door and gently banged the keys against her leg. "Will you be all right?" she asked, her gaze settling softly on Clara.

"I promise not to kill myself, if that's what you're worried about," Clara snapped, sharper than she had intended.

Randi cleared her throat and jangled the keys. "I just meant . . ."

Clara sighed. "I know what you meant, but you don't have to worry. There won't be a repeat performance."

"Okay," Randi said before turning and walking out. A few minutes later Clara heard an engine roar to life and saw a black Jeep drive away.

She sat staring around the room. Dirty dishes were left from last night, Randi's bed hadn't been made and the couch hadn't been cleared. She got up and began doing the things that were familiar to her. She had finished cleaning the bathroom when she again noticed the two doors across the hallway.

18

Curious, she opened one and found a utility room that contained the usual clutter that always seems to accumulate. Opening the other door, she caught her breath. The walls of the small room were filled with paintings. They were all watercolors of land and seascapes except for one — an oil portrait of a woman. She had long, glossy-black hair and startling blue eyes that seemed to twinkle with laughter. The painting exuded such a blatant sexuality that Clara found herself growing slightly aroused. She stood transfixed by the painting for several minutes before the signature, *RK 1988*, in the bottom left corner of the portrait caught her attention. Randi had painted this.

Intrigued, she crossed the room to a table that held several framed photographs. She picked up one that revealed several women laughing and waving at the invisible photographer. Choosing another one, she recognized the woman in the painting. She was standing with her head thrown back in laughter, and her arm securely around Randi's waist. Further examination of the photos showed the laughing woman and Randi in most of them. All of the shots were of women. Clara wondered briefly about them, and then, feeling like an intruder, she returned to the kitchen.

The sun shining through the window caught her attention. The dark skies had cleared. She took a light jacket from her suitcase and went outside. She stood looking toward the water for several seconds; the crash of the waves no longer beckoned her. A cold chill ran through her body as she recalled the false sense of peace she had felt just before Randi had pulled her from the water. Deliberately, she

19

turned her face to the warm sun and began walking away from the water.

Clara was sitting on the porch when Randi returned from Corpus.

"Hi," Randi called cheerfully, shutting off the motor and getting out of the Jeep. "How was your day?"

"All right," Clara assured her and went to help with the bags that Randi was removing. Under the groceries were several packages from an art supply store and a stack of canvases.

"You paint?" Clara cringed at the stupidity of her question. *If the woman has a stack of canvases and supplies, she obviously paints*, she chided herself. Besides, after her morning of snooping, she already knew that Randi painted.

Randi shrugged before replying. "Nothing serious. I do a few small things to sell to the tourists."

They took the groceries inside, and Clara stood by the sink looking on while Randi unpacked them. She found herself watching Randi's hands as she moved about putting away the groceries. Her thoughts kept straying to the portrait. Who was the woman? Randi cut into her reverie and held up a package of steaks and a bottle of wine.

"It's been a while since I've had company. I thought we'd celebrate. Since it's so warm outside, why don't we barbecue?" She stopped abruptly, a small frown appearing. "I never thought to ask. Are you a vegetarian?"

Clara shook her head.

"I sometimes forget that not everyone has my bad habits," she said, stuffing the empty bags into the trash can. Randi straightened up and glanced around the room for the first time. "You cleaned and even made my bed. You didn't have to do that." Looking embarrassed she added, "I've lived alone so long, I've turned into a real slob."

"It gave me something to do. It's a habit after all those years of..." The sentence trailed off.

Randi quickly covered the awkward silence. "I have to get the rest of the stuff out of the Jeep, and then I'm going to go work for a while."

Clara followed her back outside and helped carry in the items from the art supply store. They stacked everything by the empty easel in front of the bay window.

Randi raised up and stretched. "I'm going to change and go see if I can find a bird."

"A bird?"

"Yeah. I've been commissioned to do a series of twelve watercolors of shore birds for the South Texas Exhibit, and I've only got a month to complete them."

"Twelve. Isn't that a lot of work to do in a month?"

"Yeah. I was second choice. The guy they originally commissioned got sick or something. That's why I have a short deadline, which also raised my commission." Randi wriggled her eyebrows and smiled. "Twelve paintings would be impossible, but twelve pictures of birds is a piece of cake. Or should I say a pie? Of course, that was twelve and twenty blackbirds."

Confused, Clara frowned. Randi cleared her throat

21

and headed toward the bathroom. She came back stuffing the tail of a faded-blue work shirt into a pair of paint-smeared jeans. "I'm not temperamental. Why don't you go with me?"

"I'd get in your way," she said, watching Randi tuck the shirt in.

"No, you won't. Come on. You can help me choose which ones to paint. I don't know the first thing about birds. With my luck I'll end up with twelve pictures of the same bird." Randi was rummaging through the boxes that were stacked around the easel. She threw pencils and a sketch pad into a cotton bag and picked up a large case. Sliding the handles of the bag on her shoulder, she grabbed the easel. "Bring one of those smaller canvases," she said, pointing to the stack near the wall.

Somewhat reluctantly, Clara followed her to the Jeep.

"Pile in and hang on."

Randi hummed an old Beatles tune as they drove slowly along the beach. It took her several minutes, but she eventually selected a group of birds feeding at the edge of the water. After parking several yards away, she took out her bag and a sketch pad and pulled a pair of binoculars from under the seat. She hoisted herself onto the fender, settled the pad on her knee, and began to sketch.

Clara sat with the door of the Jeep open and watched Randi work, glad that she had agreed to come.

CHAPTER FOUR

Clara sat lost in thought. Her life with Allen was over — that much she was certain of. The only question remaining was what her relationship with her sons would be. If they wanted to live with her, would Allen allow it? How would she support them? For that matter, how was she going to support herself? There'd been a time when she had dreamed of a career in journalism. She had been editor of her high school paper and had worked part-time doing odd jobs for the *Shreveport Herald* during college.

They'd even published some of her work, but that had been so long ago. What could she do now?

She studied Randi's profile while Randi sketched the feeding birds. The strong, tanned hand moved with a sense of certainty. What would it be like to have that kind of confidence in your abilities?

Clara turned to gaze at the beauty around her and found herself caught up in the rhythm of the tide. Suddenly she became extremely aware of her surroundings. She gasped, trying to comprehend what was happening. Colors became more brilliant, and she was acutely aware of even the tiniest details. She could smell the oil and gasoline from the Jeep's engine. Her fingertips were able to distinguish the individual strands of fiber in the seat covering. Her silk stockings whispered sensually against her legs, and she could taste the salt on her lips. Sounds filled her ears: the clicking of the cooling engine, the sharp rasping of Randi's pencil against the paper, the hiss of the water as it rolled to the shoreline, and the shrill piping of the birds' calls. She froze, absorbing every detail of her surroundings. When the sensations faded she felt weak. Clara leaned against the seat, shocked by the realization that she very much wanted to live. It hadn't been her life she had wanted to end, just her life with Allen.

She glanced over at Randi. "Thank you for being there," she murmured, and laughed silently. *This is the point in the movies where I should break into a song*. She giggled to herself. Unable to remain still, she slid from the seat and walked around to stand next to Randi. "Mind if I watch?"

"Only if you promise not to laugh," Randi murmured.

Glancing at the pad, Clara was amazed to see that Randi had already sketched in the water and skyline and was deftly adding a bird. After a few minutes, she exclaimed, "It's a killdeer!"

With pencil posed in mid-stroke Randi stopped and looked at her. "What?"

"The bird," Clara answered shyly, afraid her outburst had disturbed her. "It's a killdeer."

Randi glanced at the sketch and back to Clara. "You actually know what kind of bird this is?"

"I'm sorry. Maybe I should just take a walk." She turned to leave.

"Wait a minute." Randi slid off the fender and brushed back a lock of hair that was constantly falling down on her forehead. "Do you know something about birds?"

Clara shrugged. "A little."

"I'm really worried about this commission. In fact, I almost turned it down. The truth is, I don't know one bird from another. If it has feathers and a beak, I consider it a bird. Maybe you could help me?" Randi suggested.

"I don't know anything about painting," Clara replied, her arms hugging her waist. Why hadn't she just stayed in the Jeep? There was no need to advertise her ignorance.

"You don't have to," Randi said, shaking her head. "If you can identify birds, you can make sure I don't paint twelve of these killdoers."

"Killdeers."

"Oh. Well, see?" Randi waved her hand as if to emphasize her point. "How about it? Will you agree to be my technical consultant?"

Clara hesitated. She should be leaving. She had to

start establishing a life of her own, but she still had no idea where she would go.

"I'll give you ten percent of my commission on the series," Randi offered.

"You don't have to pay me," Clara answered, stunned. "It's just that ... I should be leaving."

"I understand." Clara sensed Randi's disappointment as she hopped back on the fender and picked up her binoculars.

Clara walked away from the Jeep and strolled for several minutes before gathering her skirt under her and settling down on the sand. She recalled the biology project she had helped Jamie with on classifying the families of birds. They'd spent weeks going to the library, the zoo, and a local park to research and study various birds. That was how she'd learned to distinguish the different groups.

More than an hour later, Randi walked toward her. There was a sureness and confidence in the way she moved that Clara envied. Randi handed her a small canvas.

"What do you think about this?" Randi asked as she dropped into the sand next to Clara and stretched out. "Be careful. It's still wet." She lit two cigarettes and handed one to Clara.

Holding the canvas carefully by its sides, Clara stared in amazement. The sketches had been good, but the birds in the painting looked as though they should take flight from the canvas. "How did you finish so quickly?"

Randi flicked ashes from her cigarette. "Painting a bird doesn't require much creative thinking." She blew a stream of smoke that rapidly disintegrated in the wind. "I thought it would be a nice touch to put the male and female both in one setting."

Clara studied the painting and frowned. *Do I dare tell her?*

"Why are you frowning? Did I get the colors wrong or something?" Randi leaned closer to re-examine the canvas.

Clara could feel the heat of Randi's body on her arm. It felt strangely comforting. "No, I believe the colors are fine. It's just that you have two different types of birds here."

"Yeah. A male and a female. See? One has dull colors and the other has brighter colors. I know that much about birds."

She glanced at Randi and saw the glint of uncertainty in her eyes.

"What do I have?" Randi asked, defeated.

"You do have a male and a female," Clara said, "but one is a killdeer and the other is a semipalmated plover."

Randi groaned dramatically and clutched her head. "My career is ruined! At the age of forty-five, I'll be forced to return to the real world and join that eight-to-five madhouse."

Clara couldn't stop the laughter that bubbled from her.

"I'll just call the commission and confess my ignorance." Randi groaned and dropped back into the sand. She looked at Clara with arched eyebrows. "If only there was someone I could turn to for help. Then maybe I could salvage my career."

"Randi, I would but —"

Randi jumped to her knees before Clara could

finish. "I'll work night and day. I won't even take time to eat. I'll finish in two weeks."

"Two weeks!"

"Okay, thirteen days. I don't need a lot of sleep."

Clara laughed again. "It's not the time."

"Then what's the problem?"

Clara turned her gaze back to the painting. "It's just that . . . I have no place . . . what I mean is . . ."

"Oh, I know." Randi stood and stepped away before brushing the sand from her pants. "You're holding out for the bed. You're tired of sleeping on that lumpy old couch, and you're holding my career hostage."

Clara shook her head and looked up into the teasing gray eyes.

"You're taking advantage of my ignorance, madam," Randi scolded, offering her hand. "Well," she grunted pulling Clara up. "You win. I'm in desperate trouble. Without your help I'm going to have my plovers eating with my sparrows. God," she groaned, "you drive a hard bargain."

Clara smiled and said, "Let's make a deal. I'll help you in exchange for room and board. And you keep your bed." She knew she was just postponing having to make a decision.

"Now you're feeling sorry for me."

"No, it's just that I owe you," Clara replied seriously.

"You don't owe me anything. I saw the perfect opportunity to help a damsel in distress."

Clara recalled the picture of Randi and the black-haired woman and realized she was still holding Randi's hand. She reluctantly let it go and took a last drag on her cigarette before smashing it out in the sand. "I'm glad you were there," Clara admitted as her gaze locked with Randi's. She shuddered at the slight tingling sensation that ran through her.

Randi suddenly shifted her weight to one foot and looked away. "Let's get back to the house and get those steaks on. I'm starving."

When they pulled up to the house, Randi nodded to the painting Clara was holding. "You can pitch that on the scrap heap. We'll start over tomorrow."

"Pitch it!"

"Yeah. Tomorrow you can help me find another group. I'll paint it instead of one of those semipalmated whatchamacallits."

"But this one is too pretty to simply pitch." She stared at the painting in her hand. "Would you mind if I kept it?" she asked hesitantly.

Randi looked at her strangely. "No, of course not."

After they unloaded the Jeep, Randi went outside through a door at the back of the utility room that Clara hadn't noticed in her earlier exploration. Clara followed her and found a rather large patio. "This is nice."

"I helped build it," Randi said proudly, uncovering the barbecue pit.

"You're joking."

"No. About five years ago I bought this place as a weekend retreat, and a friend helped me build the patio."

Clara recalled the painting again. "Does your friend live near here?"

"No," Randi answered rather abruptly. She poured in the charcoal and started the fire before going back into the house.

Clara stood watching wind chimes perform a peaceful dance from the limb of an ancient oak that was a few yards from the patio. What would it be like to have her own place with no one around to make decisions for her? A slight smile crossed her lips at the thought of such freedom.

By the time Randi returned, the charcoal had burned down. She added more starter fluid and dropped in a match. The flames emitted a loud whoosh and licked greedily through the grill.

"Would you mind putting the steaks on when the fire's ready? It's getting late, and I'd like to run before it gets dark."

"Go ahead. I'll watch them."

Randi left, and a few minutes later Clara saw her jogging down the road in a black T-shirt and gray shorts.

Clara went inside to make a salad. She wondered about the boys. Were they getting along all right? Did they miss her? Going to the phone by the bed, she punched in the number. Allen answered.

"Where the hell are you?" he snapped as soon as he heard her voice.

"I'm fine, Allen. Thanks for your concern. How are the boys?"

"They're fine."

"Can I talk to them?"

"They're not here. They've gone to a movie."

"I can see everyone's worried about me," she said dryly.

"They're just kids. What do you think you're doing anyway? Leaving a note here saying you had to get away, not telling me where you're going. Don't you think you're a little old to be out *finding* yourself?"

"I've left you."

"Why?"

Clara detected the faint surprise in his voice. "How many reasons do you need?" She ran her hand across Randi's pillow.

"One good one."

"Nancy, Wilma, Angel . . ."

"All right, all right," he growled, "but why now?"

"The boys are older. They don't need me anymore."

"Of course they need you. How are they supposed to get up and get to school? What about their meals? What am I supposed to do about that dinner for the sales reps next week?"

"Hire a maid." She hung up and went back to preparing the salad.

Seeing the bottle of wine on the counter, she started looking for something to chill it in. All she could find was a small, plastic cleaning bucket. Rinsing it out, she laughed at the thought of how Allen would have reacted had she ever served him wine chilled in a plastic bucket. Allen's family was from old money. Even though the family fortune had long since disappeared, they never admitted that the money no longer existed. There were certain standards that were or were not acceptable. Clara grinned. Collecting two jelly glasses, she carried them and the wine outside to the picnic table. Chilling wine in a plastic bucket would definitely fit under the "not acceptable" column. By the time Randi returned, Clara had prepared even more food and was ready to put on the steaks.

"Hey," Randi said, sniffing as she came in. "Something smells good in here."

"I decided to add scalloped potatoes and a salad to your menu. Hope you don't mind."

"No, that's great, but what's that smell?"

"A chocolate cake."

"Chocolate cake! You found one in this house?" Randi's eyes closed as she inhaled deeply.

Clara chuckled and said, "It was pretty well hidden, but I managed to scrape together everything I needed for it."

"Let me get a shower, and I'll be out to help you," she called, racing off toward the bathroom.

Clara found a tablecloth in one of the drawers beneath the sink. By the time Randi had finished her shower, Clara was taking the steaks off the grill.

Randi walked out onto the darkening patio and whistled. "Now this is what I call a meal." Clara had set the food on the picnic table. Randi flipped a switch, and a string of gaily-colored patio lights blinked on, bathing them in a soft warm glow.

Clara turned to find Randi standing behind her. Her breath caught as the faint sensation ran through her stomach again. Their gaze locked. "I couldn't find a corkscrew," Clara said uncertainly.

"I'll get it," Randi murmured as she turned sharply away.

* * * * *

32

Clara pushed her plate back and moaned. "I'm stuffed."

"The meal was delicious," Randi said as she lit a cigarette and handed Clara the pack. Their fingers brushed slightly in the exchange. "My compliments to the chef."

Clara felt an almost adolescent flush of pride and bent her head in embarrassment. "Thank you."

Randi refilled their glasses. "By the way. I meant to congratulate you on your choice of ice buckets."

"It's all I could find," Clara admitted. "What do you normally use?"

"I'm short on social graces. I just take it in and out of the refrigerator," Randi declared.

Clara stood and started clearing the table.

"Sit down," Randi insisted. "You cooked; I'll clean up."

"I don't mind," she said. Allen would never dream of helping clear the table. He had definite ideas on what was and wasn't his responsibility.

"Well, I do. Sit down. I'll be right back." Randi gathered a handful of dishes and disappeared into the house. She soon returned carrying two chaise longues. Setting them up, she said, "Have a seat. I'll be done in a few minutes." She disappeared into the house again.

Clara moved the chairs to the edge of the patio so she could see the sky. A full moon had risen and filled the night with soft golden light. Sighing, she relaxed into the chair and gazed at the sky. Stars were beginning to pop out. She tried to recall how long it had been since she'd felt this good. Had she ever been this relaxed? Maybe right after she and Allen had met.

They had been introduced at a party when she was a junior in college. Clara had been almost painfully shy, and Allen had made her feel so rare and special. Two months later they were married. He had worked for a prosperous appliance retailer where he had eventually worked himself up to vice president of marketing. While they were dating he'd been gentle and caring and had encouraged her to build a career, but once they were married it was a different story.

They didn't have the money for her to continue with college, and Allen wouldn't allow her father to keep paying her tuition. At the time it had seemed so mature of him to want to provide for her. She had bought into society's picture of the happy housewife staying at home and caring for her husband. Besides, they had agreed that she could return to school when they were more financially secure. She had continued writing and had sold an occasional piece despite Allen's protests. Then Jamie was born, and she discovered she had much less time and energy. Two years later Roger was born, and Clara reluctantly gave up her dream of returning to college and gradually locked away her hopes of a career in journalism.

Somewhere in that time frame, Allen began telling her she was incompetent and too slow to compete with the outside world. He told her so often that she eventually began to believe it. During the last few years it had been Belinda's support and encouragement that had kept Clara from completely losing her mind. Guilt flooded through her. She hadn't thought of Belinda since before leaving Shreveport. She jumped up and went inside.

"I thought you were relaxing," Randi said, drying her hands. "I put on a pot of coffee. It'll go great with the cake."

"Could I use your phone?"

"Sure. I'm finished here. I'll just take this cake to keep me company. Bring the coffee out when you're ready." She gathered up the cake and left.

As soon as she was alone, Clara dialed Belinda's number.

"Clara!" Belinda's concern showed in her voice. "Are you all right? Allen called looking for you. I've been worried sick. Where are you?"

"Slow down," she said with a slight sense of gratitude that someone had missed her. "I'm fine. I'm about forty-five miles from Corpus Christi."

"Texas!"

"Yes." She laughed to herself, remembering Randi's crack about the last survey. "I've left Allen. I'm staying with a friend for a few days."

"What are you going to do then?" Belinda asked after a slight pause.

"I don't know. I need some time alone."

"I understand. But, Clara, keep in touch. I miss you." There was a slight catch in her voice that brought tears to Clara's eyes.

"I will. I miss you too." Clara gave her the phone number that was on the front of the phone and said good-bye. She stared for several minutes at the receiver. Belinda had been the anchoring point of her life for the past few years.

She took two cups of coffee out to the patio where Randi sat bathed in the moon's reflection.

"Do you want the lights back on?" Randi asked.

"No, it's too beautiful." She placed the coffee

between them. "It's been ages since I've been able to enjoy sitting out like this."

"Where did you learn so much about birds?"

Clara didn't answer, and so Randi handed her a plate. "This cake is delicious." Clara looked over to see a large chunk missing and smiled to herself. They were silent as they ate cake and finished their coffee.

Afterward, Randi took out a cigarette and offered the pack to her. Randi struck a match and held it out. Clara's hand gently cupped Randi's as she steadied the match's flame. Clara couldn't help but notice the soft texture of Randi's hand. As the cigarette caught, Randi pulled away and was about to light her own when Clara spoke.

"Randi, are you a lesbian?" Clara could see the shocked expression on Randi's face. The match must have burned her finger, because she blew it out quickly and rubbed her fingertip against her jeans. She slowly took the cigarette from her mouth.

"Yes, I am. Is that a problem for you?" There was a touch of defiance in her voice that caused Clara to close her eyes and rub her temples. Why had she blurted it out like that?

"No. I'm sorry I asked. I should've minded my own business. I just —"

"You thought I was a love-starved old maid who had invited you to stay so that I could prey upon you," Randi said as she struck another match roughly and lit her cigarette.

"No. It's just that, well, while you were out this morning I was nosy. I went into the other room and noticed the pictures of you and that other woman."

Randi shrugged and smoked her cigarette silently.

"I shouldn't have abused your trust. I'm sorry."

36

"Don't worry about it."

"You haven't questioned me," Clara said. "Even after . . . after pulling me out of the water."

Randi rubbed her forehead. "If it makes you feel any better, I know your car is registered to Allen Webster of Shreveport, Louisiana. Your driver's license shows the same last name and the same address and you carry a photo of two young boys that bear a striking resemblance to you. I went through your wallet yesterday."

Looking at each other in the moonlight, they burst out laughing.

"Well," Clara said, "so much for trust and faith. I think I could use another glass of wine." She started to rise. Randi's hand on her arm stopped her.

"Sit still. I'll get some clean glasses." Flinging the cigarette away, Randi went inside.

Clara sat staring at the moon, wondering about the woman with the long dark hair. Had she been Randi's lover? What had happened to her? What would it be like to make love to a woman? A rush of warmth swept over her.

"Here you go." Randi's voice interrupted her thoughts. She held out a glass of wine. When Clara reached for the glass, she was shocked to find her hands were trembling.

"I guess I owe you an explanation," Clara said as they sat sipping their wine.

"Only if you want to tell me. To be honest, it's been nice having someone around to talk to again."

"I did wonder why you live way out here by yourself."

"I've only been living here for about a year. Until then I lived in Corpus. When I decided to start painting again, I thought this would be a better place to work than my studio in Corpus," Randi explained and sipped her wine.

"Who is the woman in the painting?" Clara asked tentatively.

"Liz."

"Was she your . . ." she stopped, wondering what the appropriate term was.

"You're downright bashful, aren't you?" Randi teased.

"This may sound sadistic, but it's nice to know I'm not the only person with problems. I've been so closed off from the world that it sometimes seems that I'm the only one."

"You'll soon find that everyone has their share of problems. But to answer your question, yes, she was my lover."

"What happened?" Clara asked, somehow knowing it was all right to ask.

"She left. No, that's not exactly true. I drove her away," Randi said. "My career as an artist exploded into high gear practically overnight. Suddenly I had more offers than I could possibly accept. There were parties everywhere, and everyone wanted to talk to the brilliant new artist. It all went to my head." She took a sip of wine before continuing. "The exhibits started, and I was away more than I was home. Liz wasn't able to travel with me very often. She's an architect and worked with one of the firms in Corpus. They were receiving a lot of federal contracts at the time, and she stayed pretty busy." She brushed a hand through her hair. "It reached the point that when I was home, I was restless, dreaming of the next party. Liz got tired. Someone else started being there when I should've been and gave her the attention she needed." Randi's voice shook with emotion. She took a deep breath and slowly exhaled.

Clara wanted to take her hand, but she wasn't sure how Randi would interpret the gesture.

Randi's voice was lower when she began speaking again. "By the time I realized what was happening, it was too late. I tried everything to get her back, but nothing worked. When Liz left, I came apart and couldn't paint anymore. The colors either wouldn't mix or they all ran together into an ungodly mess. So I left the real world and curled up with a bottle of Scotch. I spent several months feeling sorry for myself until a couple of very good friends finally stepped in and literally kicked me back into the world of the living. Once I was out there, I realized I was ready to try again." She sighed and shrugged. "I plan on staying here until I can get an exhibit together."

"How many paintings have you completed since you came back?" Clara asked.

"None." The silence hung between them.

"Why not?"

Randi sipped her wine before answering. "Something isn't right. I'm still missing something."

"I'm sorry about Liz."

"Don't be. It was my own stupidity." Randi looked at Clara. "You're taking this rather calmly. You don't mind being all alone with a lesbian?"

"I don't think I have anything to fear from you," Clara admitted. "Besides, you stopped me from doing something I didn't really want to do."

"So why did you try?"

Clara shrugged. How could she explain that

39

moment of insanity to Randi when she couldn't even explain it to herself? She took a deep breath and slowly exhaled before speaking. "At the time it seemed like the only thing left to do." She paused and took a drink. "I woke up one morning and realized I'd been kidding myself. The boys — I have two sons, Jamie, seventeen, and Roger, fifteen — don't need me for anything other than clean clothes and an occasional meal. Allen, my husband, hasn't needed or wanted me in years." Her voice dropped slightly. "He's had plenty of secretaries, salesclerks, and business associates to keep him happy." She leaned her head back on the chair and stared at the sky. "I couldn't take it any longer." When Randi didn't respond she added, "You must think I'm terrible for leaving my children."

"No. I think we have to learn to take care of ourselves before we can care for others." She looked at Clara and smiled. "I guess that's what we're both learning to do."

"You sound like my friend Belinda. She always kept me on track." She gave a weak, humorless laugh. "Allen never liked Belinda. She's been married and divorced three times." Clara set her glass between the chairs. Randi was lying back in the chaise longue looking at her.

"Belinda says she married the first time to get away from home, the second time to get out of loneliness, and the third time to get security, but that from now on she intends to live for lust."

"Sounds to me like she should've given them all up for a good woman," Randi observed.

Clara looked startled.

"Sorry. I was teasing."

"Why are you, I mean, why do you . . . ?"

"Prefer women?"

"Yes." Clara laughed nervously.

"I don't really know. Why does one person prefer brunets while another prefers blonds?"

"Am I being rude?" Clara asked.

"I'll let you know if you are," Randi assured her and smiled, taking the sting out of the words. "But we were talking about you."

"There's really nothing else to tell. I reached a point to where I couldn't face it any longer. I got up one morning, wrote Allen a note, and left. I finally worked up the courage to call home today, and he was only concerned about the dinner party he is supposed to give. The boys were at a movie." Tears spilled down her cheeks.

"Allen's a fool," Randi growled and lit more cigarettes. They sat smoking in silence for several minutes.

"Tell me something else about yourself," Clara said, turning her head toward Randi.

"Well, I'm an only child. My parents were both in their thirties when I was born. They had already given up on being able to have kids."

"A miracle baby," Clara said.

"I don't know about that. I was such a hell-raiser I'm sure that opinion would have changed quickly, had they ever thought so."

"I can't believe you were that bad," Clara teased.

"I was a tomboy." Randi sighed and stretched out. "My parents thought it was cute until I got to be around twelve, and then suddenly Mom began to buy me all of these dresses." Randi chuckled. "Can't you just imagine me in a dress?"

"I'll bet you were cute," Clara said softly.

Randi made a noise that closely resembled a snort. "Right. I'd hide the dresses as fast as she'd buy them. The older I got, the worse it became. I had no idea what was wrong with me. I only knew that I couldn't be like the other girls. Then when I was sixteen I met Maridale Hart." Randi playfully placed both hands over her heart and moaned. "Are you sure you're ready to hear about my torrid romances?" she asked, looking at Clara.

"I think I can handle it," Clara answered playfully. "How did you meet her?"

"Her father had just been transferred to Corpus. He worked for a gas company or something. The first time I laid eyes on her I almost came in my seat. Oh, sorry." She glanced at Clara, who was intently studying her glass of wine. Randi cleared her throat. "Anyway, you get the picture."

"I'm trying not to," Clara offered quietly, both amused and embarrassed.

"It took me two weeks to finally get the courage to talk to her. I invited her to a movie. It was the best night of my life." Randi stared into the moonlit night.

"What happened?" Clara asked impatiently.

"You won't believe me if I tell you. No one ever does."

"Yes I will. What happened?"

"Well the movie was about halfway through when she reached over and took my hand and put it on her knee. Lord almighty, my heart just about burst through my chest," Randi groaned.

"What happened then?" Clara asked, leaning slightly forward, caught up in Randi's story.

"I woke up."

"What?"

"I had fallen asleep in the movie and was dreaming. She woke me up to leave. But I knew right then and there what it was I wanted."

"You!" Clara reached across to smack Randi's shoulder just as Randi leaped from her chair. Clara scrambled up and ran after her. "I believed you," she yelled as they raced around the oak tree.

"It's all true," Randi said, laughing as she darted away from the tree. Randi slipped on the grass and Clara caught her before she could reach the patio. They tumbled into the grass laughing and rolling.

Clara attempted to pin Randi down, but Randi gave a sharp twist that sent Clara rolling backward. Without warning, Randi was sitting over her and pinning Clara's arms to the ground. Their faces were only inches apart. The world seemed to stand still for Clara as she gazed at the smooth softness of Randi's mouth. The moonlight gave enough illumination for Clara to see Randi's gaze drilling into her. Randi's breath brushed softly against her cheek as Randi's face drew slowly closer. Clara knew Randi was going to kiss her, and she knew she wasn't going to resist. She fought to control her breathing as her heart pounded with anticipation. Suddenly Randi was standing and pulling Clara up beside her. Dazed, Clara could only stare at her.

"It's getting late." Randi's voice sounded odd. "I'll see you in the morning."

"Wait." Clara reached to touch her arm. "What happened with Maridale?" She couldn't believe she had asked the question when what she had wanted to say was — was what? she wondered.

"She liked boys. I spent the rest of the evening listening to her talk about this guy she was crazy about."

"I'm sorry," Clara said sincerely, feeling the pain the young Randi must have experienced.

Randi shrugged. She started to turn away, but stopped and smiled mischievously. "Wait until you hear about Rhonda."

Clara's laughter eased the tension between them as they went into the house.

CHAPTER FIVE

During the next two weeks Randi completed the paintings for the South Texas Exhibit with Clara's help. She also did several small seascapes, which she sold at a local roadside tourist stop. When Randi wasn't working on the paintings of the birds, Clara stayed at the house to read or sit by the water. The circles under her eyes disappeared, and she grew tan and began to laugh more. She often found herself wondering about her feelings for Randi. She had no point of reference for comparison. Maybe this was how women related to each other. She had never had a really close friend — other than Belinda, she reminded herself. But even Belinda had always seemed slightly aloof and reserved around her. As if there was a part of herself she never allowed Clara to see.

Clara had never experienced passion. She had rarely dated in high school and had been a virgin when she married Allen. His attention had flattered her, and he offered a sense of security. She supposed in the beginning she had loved him, or maybe she had just been infatuated with him.

Randi and Clara had both been politely careful with each other since the night of the barbecue. Clara sometimes found herself wondering if she hadn't imagined the entire episode. Often when Randi was working alone, Clara would pack sandwiches and take them to her so they could enjoy lunch together. Dinner was a joint effort. They quickly settled into a comfortable routine.

They were watching television after dinner when the phone rang. After answering it, Randi returned to the couch and waited for a commercial to begin before she spoke.

"That was a couple of friends. How would you like to go into Corpus tomorrow and spend the weekend?"

"I don't think so," Clara answered shyly.

"I need to go in and deliver the paintings for the South Texas Exhibit. Come on," Randi coaxed. "It'll be fun." When Clara didn't answer right away, she continued. "They have plenty of room for us, and it'll do you good to get out and meet people." She stretched her legs. "I guess I should warn you that they're lesbians." She rushed on before Clara could answer. "I've already told them you weren't, and they promised they wouldn't hold it against you."

Clara turned to protest but saw that Randi was teasing her.

"Think you're funny, don't you?" she said and tossed a pillow at her.

"Say you'll go, and I'll hush so you can watch the movie in peace."

Clara looked at her for a second before sighing. The stray lock of hair had fallen across Randi's forehead. Clara smoothed it back without thinking. As her fingers slid through the dark strands, a jolt shot through her. She heard her own sharp intake of breath. Randi's cheeks had become two glowing orbs. Clara quickly pulled away and turned her attention to the crackling fire. Several seconds passed before she was able to speak. "All right, but only if you're sure they won't mind."

"They won't. I've already told them you'll come."

Clara could tell by the sound of Randi's voice that she was teasing her. She hadn't seemed to notice Clara's discomfort.

"Mighty sure of yourself, weren't you?" Clara asked, certain Randi could hear the tremor in her voice. Randi turned to look at her.

"Women never turn me down," she replied, her eyes smoldering.

Embarrassed and confused by the flood of

emotions rushing through her, Clara tossed the remaining pillow at her. "Be quiet. I'm trying to concentrate on this movie."

Early the next day, Clara began to sort through her clothes and choose what she wanted to take. She was sitting on the couch staring at the pile when Randi came in.

"What are you doing?" she asked, staring at the jumble of clothing.

"I was just thinking. It's been three years since I've bought a new dress." Turning, she looked at Randi. "Could we go in early? I want to go shopping."

"Sure. Let me pack some clothes and load the paintings."

Twenty minutes later they were on their way to Corpus. Clara felt like a schoolgirl on her first field trip.

She waited in the Jeep while Randi dropped off the paintings. The sun felt warm shining through the windows. Now that Randi had finished the series on birds, there was no reason for Clara to stay. Clara knew she should be thinking about her future and what she was going to do, but she didn't want to spoil her day.

Randi came out of the building grinning and waving a check. Clara found herself smiling in return.

Several minutes later, they parked in front of a large department store. Clara's eyes greedily devoured the spring fashions in the window.

"Well, are you going to sit there all day or are we going in?" Randi called from the sidewalk.

Clara had a hundred dollars left and decided not to spend more than fifty of it. She didn't want to think about what she would do when she had to leave.

The store was full of beautiful clothes. How was she ever going to decide what to choose?

"What do you want to look at first?"

"I don't know," Clara answered nervously.

"Let's narrow it down: dresses, pants, shorts."

"I could never wear pants or shorts! I'm too fat."

"Fat!" Randi echoed with a stunned look.

"The last time I bought a pair of pants Allen made me take them back. He said I looked like a washer woman."

"That's bullshit. And besides, I for one find fat washer women sexy," Randi said and grabbed her arm, leading her quickly through the racks of clothing. "Tell me if you see anything you like."

"You'll have to slow down. I can't see," she said breathlessly. Her mind was racing over Randi's statement. Did Randi think she was sexy? She didn't have time to dwell on the thought, because Randi's enthusiastic rush across the store required her full attention.

When they stopped they were in front of a long rack of pants. Randi was taking down different styles and colors.

"What are you doing?"

"We're shopping," Randi replied.

"Randi, I can't wear those."

"Why not?" She looked at Clara and wriggled her

eyebrows. "Trust me." Grabbing Clara's arm, she hauled her across the store toward a dressing room.

"How many?" the salesclerk drawled as she admitted them.

Randi quickly counted. "Eight."

"Sorry. Only three items per customer."

"All right. Three." Randi thrust three pairs of pants at Clara and kept three herself. "Here." She handed the two remaining items to the clerk. "You hold on to these."

They found an empty dressing booth. "Try them on," Randi said, "and when you find a pair that fits, let me know."

Clara was looking at the labels. "Randi, they're all too small. I couldn't possibly fit into any of these."

"Just try them."

Clara closed the door to the dressing room. She could hear Randi humming patiently outside the tiny cubicle. She removed her skirt and pulled the pants on over her girdle. She stared down in disbelief and threw the door open to find a somewhat startled Randi. "Look! They're too big," Clara exclaimed.

Randi smiled and handed her another pair. "Try these. They're smaller. And Clara . . ." She paused.

"Yes?"

"Why don't you take that damn girdle off? It reminds me of my grandmother."

Blushing, Clara looked down at her stomach. "But Allen said —"

"Screw Allen."

"Oh," Clara said and grimaced. "That doesn't sound at all appealing." Their loud laughter caused the disapproving salesclerk to poke her head inside the corridor.

After finding the size she needed, Clara returned to the racks and began picking out various items. Each time she found something she liked they left it with the salesclerk to hold.

She tried on jeans, dresses, shorts, blouses, anything that looked interesting. After two hours, a modest stack had accumulated beside a very displeased salesclerk.

"Randi," Clara whispered. "I can't possibly afford all of this stuff."

"But it was fun looking, wasn't it?"

"How am I ever going to choose something from all of that?"

Randi didn't answer right away. She was staring at the back of a nearby cash register.

"Clara, do you have a Visa or MasterCard?"

"Yes. Both as a matter of fact." She turned and saw a wicked sparkle in Randi's eyes.

"I'll bet they're both in Allen's name, aren't they?" Randi asked.

"Randi," she said slowly, "what are you thinking?"

Randi pointed to the Visa and MasterCard emblems pasted on the back of the cash register and smiled.

Clara exclaimed, "He'd have a coronary!"

"So? How many gifts do you suppose he's bought over the years for his *associates*?"

Clara's face clouded for a second. "Miss," she called to the clerk. "I'll take everything. I'll be back shortly." She tugged Randi's arm. "Come on."

"Now what?"

"I need shoes."

"God help me. I've created a monster," Randi moaned.

51

* * * * *

An hour and a half later, they left the store with
a now smiling salesclerk trailing behind them. Everyone was laden with bags. Randi's feet were encased
in a gleaming pair of white sneakers. Clara had
insisted on purchasing them to replace the one Randi
had lost while rescuing her.

Inside the Jeep, Clara began to laugh. "Oh," she
cried. "I feel so good. I want to put something new
on and go get something to eat. I'm starved."

Randi found a service station and waited while
Clara changed. She emerged wearing white slacks, a
mint green blouse, and sandals. She twirled around
while Randi whistled and applauded. Grinning, Clara
dropped her old clothing into a garbage can — girdle
and all. She crawled into the Jeep, smiling and
marveling at the freedom her new clothes allowed.

"One more thing," Randi said.

"What? I'm too tired to shop anymore."

"Your hair."

"What's wrong with it?" Clara's hand shot to the
severe knot.

"You should wear it down."

"I don't like it down. It bothers me."

"Then get it cut," Randi said.

Clara felt a wild streak shoot through her. An
hour later she emerged from SuperCuts with a short,
fashionable bob. She climbed into the Jeep feeling shy
but exhilarated by all these sudden changes. She
looked up to find Randi staring at her strangely.
"What's wrong now?"

"You're very beautiful."

Clara's gaze fell, and her heart pounded wildly. Randi's hand was on her arm, her thumb gently caressing Clara's skin. Clara wanted to take the hand but couldn't make herself move. To her disappointment, Randi unexpectedly cleared her throat and withdrew her hand.

"Let's go. I'm starved, too," Randi said.

Clara's arm felt unusually cold after the delicious warmth of Randi's touch. Clara refused to think about what was happening.

They stopped at a burger stand and sat at a table outside.

"Tell me about your friends we're going to see," Clara said after they had devoured most of their food.

Randi was munching on the last of her fries. "They've been together for twelve years. I've known them for about ten years. They really stood by me during my breakup with Liz. They never judged me. I'm not sure what I would've done without them." Randi ran her hand through her hair. "Lisa works as a manager for an oil refinery, and Rosie is a lawyer. They own a very nice house just outside one of those swanky suburbs. They love to play tennis, go camping, and fish." Randi looked at her watch. "They also like punctuality. I told them we'd be there by six. We're going to be late."

When they finally pulled into the driveway, Clara stared in disbelief. "This is it?"

"Kind of grabs you, doesn't it?" Randi asked.

The large ranch-style house was surrounded by several huge oaks. A tennis court was at one side, and an enormous pool peeked from behind it. Looking around she could see no other houses. "I thought you said suburbs."

Randi laughed and opened her door. "Come on, let's go in. We're late enough already."

The door of the house opened, and a melodious voice rang out. "It's about time you two showed up. We were beginning to wonder if you'd gotten a better offer."

"We wanted to make sure you had plenty of time to get the beer cold," Randi returned, throwing her arms around the woman. Clara felt a sharp twinge that bordered on jealousy at their easy affectionate display.

"You're too late," Lisa joked. "I drank it while I was waiting on you."

Clara made a quick inspection of the woman who still had her arm around Randi. "Lisa, this is Clara Webster. Clara, Lisa Corbett," Randi said, stepping away from Lisa.

"Hello." Lisa extended her hand. She was tall with an abundance of long, thick chestnut hair and had crystal-blue eyes that hinted of stubbornness. Clara guessed her to be in her late thirties. "Come on in and sit down. Rosie is on the phone. She's fighting with the phone company."

"Why?" Randi asked as she and Clara sat on a pale-blue sofa. Lisa sat in a matching chair across from them.

"They accidentally left her name out of the phone book, but they keep billing her for the additional listing. She's been marking it off every month, and they keep carrying it forward." Lisa shook her head, but Clara saw the slight smile tugging at her lips.

"She calls them monthly, and now she's threatening not to pay the bill until they get it straightened out. In turn, they're threatening to shut the phone off."

At that moment a door burst open. *"Pendejos!"* Seeing Randi and Clara, she stopped and smiled so brightly that the room seemed to light up.

"Randi," she cried. "God, you get fatter and uglier every day."

Shocked, Clara stared at them.

"And you get shorter every day. Another year and you'll be able to use the booster chairs at McDonald's."

"Oh, you've been practicing." She laughed and hugged Randi furiously.

Randi pulled away and pointed to Clara, "Clara Webster, Rosie Garcia." They shook hands.

Rosie was wearing a white, sleeveless top and jeans. The blouse looked startlingly white against her dark-copper skin and long jet-black hair. She was a couple of inches shorter than Clara's own five-seven. She sat in a recliner next to Lisa's chair.

"Anybody for a cold one?" Lisa asked. They all agreed, and she excused herself and returned a short time later with four tall glasses of beer.

"How's the work going?" Rosie asked Randi.

"Slow, but sure. I've finished the stuff for the South Texas Exhibit, thanks to my technical adviser here." She pointed to Clara and smiled.

"Another painter," Lisa moaned.

"No." Clara answered. "I just happened to know a plover from a hummingbird." She smiled at Randi's grimace.

"Do you work in the field of ornithology?" Rosie asked.

"No, I picked up bits here and there while helping my son on a biology project." Clara didn't miss the look of surprise on Lisa's face.

"You must've really cracked the whip for her to be finished already. Normally she gets bored and quits," Rosie chided.

"When did I ever not finish a commission?" Randi cried defensively.

"What about the McCorkle's family portrait?"

"You —" Randi threw her hands into the air. "Don't you dare start in on that again."

"You never finished it, did you?" Rosie persisted.

"Why didn't you finish it?" Clara asked, much to Rosie's glee.

Turning to Clara, Randi dropped her hands in defeat. "I got a call from a guy who said he'd like to commission a family portrait. So I set up a time at my studio, but he insisted it be done in his home. I refused, but he kept raising the fee until I couldn't say no." Rosie chuckled, and Randi glared at her. "Anyway," Randi continued, "on the day of the setting, I show up at this really beautiful home. This nice-looking, clean-cut guy comes to the door. He invites me in and tells me his family's in the den but they're a little nervous. He asks if I would mind waiting about five minutes before coming in so he could calm them down. I thought it sounded a little strange, but for what he was paying I didn't push it. So I stand there like an ass for five minutes and then I go into the den."

Rosie started to giggle while Lisa watched her and smiled. Randi shot them both a threatening look.

"What happened?" Clara asked.

"The jerk was sitting on the floor stark naked with a couple of dozen live chickens running around the room."

"C-h-i-c-k-e-n M-a-n!" Rosie howled with laughter, imitating the old radio special.

Clara tried not to laugh, but Rosie's laughter was contagious. Even Randi was having trouble maintaining her mock outrage. "What did you do?" Clara managed to ask.

"I called him a few choice names and left."

"You never finished the portrait," Rosie chimed in triumphantly.

Clara sat back to enjoy her beer and listen as Rosie and Randi broke into a new line of arguing. Lisa turned to Clara.

"Why don't I show you around? These two will be at it for hours."

Lisa gave Clara a tour of the house before they settled into lawn chairs in the lush backyard.

"You have a beautiful home," Clara said, watching Lisa slowly shred a leaf she had picked up.

"Thank you. Randi didn't mention you had children," Lisa stated carefully.

Clara could sense her near dislike. "I have two boys. Jamie is seventeen, and Roger is fifteen."

"They don't live with you?"

Clara took a deep breath and exhaled slowly. "They currently live with their father. We're . . ." she hesitated. What were they? *Separated* seemed too soft of a word. "Getting a divorce," she added, admitting to herself for the first time what she truly wanted.

Lisa studied the tiny remnant of leaf in her hand. "Randi means a lot to me. I wouldn't want to see

57

her get hurt again. She's been through a lot, and she's just now beginning to pull her life back together."

Clara looked up to find Lisa staring at her. Clara cleared her throat nervously before speaking. "Randi and I are just friends. She's really helped me in the last couple of weeks." Frustrated, she stopped. How could she explain everything that Randi had done for her? Giving up, she blurted, "I can't honestly say what my feelings for Randi are at this point, but I do know she's very special to me and I wouldn't want to see her hurt either."

Lisa sat watching her quietly for a moment before smiling. "I believe you."

A loud burst of laughter erupted from the back door as Rosie and Randi came out to join them.

The four women stood on the patio watching the fading sunset. Rosie's arm settled around Lisa's waist; Clara stole glances in their direction. They seemed so at ease and comfortable with each other. Lisa lightly kissed Rosie's lips. Clara swiftly averted her eyes and found Randi gazing at her. Unable to look away, Clara was shaken by the turmoil going on within her body. Her knees were shaking. *It's the beer*, she told herself. She wasn't used to drinking. The shopping had gotten her too keyed up. Tearing her eyes from Randi, she sat down on a bench and listened to the three old friends chatting.

They agreed to get an early start the next morning and go fishing. Clara had never been fishing, but with Randi assuring her what great fun they'd have, she agreed to try it. When they were ready to turn in, Lisa showed Clara to her room; Randi would be in an adjoining one. Clara was puzzled by her disappointment when she realized they wouldn't be staying together. She watched with a feeling close to jealousy as Lisa and Rosie walked hand in hand down the hallway. She lay staring at the ceiling for several hours, aching with emptiness.

The next morning they went to the marina and boarded Lisa and Rosie's boat. Clara was amazed. "It's a small yacht," she cried.

Lisa laughed. "Not quite a yacht, but it floats."

Clara watched somewhat nervously as the city's skyline disappeared from view, causing the water to merge with the sky. Randi showed her how to bait her hook and how to secure the pole in the pole clasp. Settling down in chairs that were bolted to the deck, they soon fell into a peaceful silence. The slight rock of the boat and warm sun soon lulled Clara to sleep.

A shadow fell across her. She opened her eyes to find Randi smiling down at her. Clara returned the smile. Randi extended her hand and pulled her up. Randi drew her into her arms. Clara's heart pounded as Randi's hands slowly traveled down her back until they rested on her hips. Randi leaned into Clara and let her lips graze along her cheek before moving on to explore the throbbing pulse in Clara's neck. Clara heard herself groan when Randi's hands slid slowly up her thighs. They slipped between her legs and a loud scream filled the air.

Clara jerked awake, aroused and confused. The high-pitched screaming continued. Randi and Rosie were running toward her shouting.

"You've got a big one!" Rosie yelled.

Clara turned to see her fishing pole relax. Without thinking, Clara grabbed the pole from the clasp.

"No!" Randi yelled.

It was too late. The fish had begun to dive for the safety of the water's depth. All three women clung to the pole, but Clara could feel it slipping from their hands.

"Get it back in the clasp," Rosie groaned, straining against the fighting fish.

The line screamed again. The fish soared high out of the water, causing the pole to leap forward and drag them with it. Lisa appeared from the other side of the boat and joined them. Clara's arms were beginning to ache, but still the huge fish struggled. The line suddenly went slack, and they thrust the pole back into the clasp just before the fish began to run again.

Clara collapsed into her chair shaking. It was only a dream she told herself, watching in a daze as Randi and Rosie continued to work the line, trying to reel the catch in. She turned to find Lisa watching her. Clara almost burst into tears when Lisa smiled at her softly and squeezed her shoulder. Randi excitedly snatched Clara's hand and hauled her up. "It's your catch, bring it in!"

An hour later, the enormous marlin hung suspended from a hoist. It had taken all four of them to finally wear the marlin down enough to pull it in. Exhausted, they slid to the deck.

Rosie shielded her eyes from the sun and looked proudly at the hoist. "I never thought we'd get to use it."

"What do we do with it?" Clara asked, shaking from exhaustion.

"You should have it mounted," Rosie suggested. Excitement quickly replaced their exhaustion. Randi and Rosie began to argue about which taxidermist was best and who should call the paper to report the huge catch.

Clara looked at the suspended marlin and felt a mixture of emotions tear through her. She knew what it felt like to be trapped.

"What's wrong?" Randi asked softly.

Clara looked from the marlin to the three women and back again at the poor creature. "Couldn't we just let it go?" she asked weakly.

"Let it go!" Rosie shrieked. "You don't catch a marlin that size every day. Nobody lets one go. That's —"

Lisa had laid her hand on Rosie's arm and stopped her in mid-sentence. Tears burned Clara's eyes and Rosie began to stammer.

"But . . . I . . . oh hell, there's always a first time. Besides, it's really too big to mount. Where would you hang it? A dead fish on the wall is gross anyway. Something that big would . . . uh . . ." She looked to Randi for help.

"Yeah," Randi joined in, "and we'd have to take it home in the Jeep, which is certainly too small."

"Why don't we take a picture," Lisa suggested, "and then let it go?" Lisa quickly ran below and returned with a camera. A few moments later they swung the hoist over the side and carefully released the catch of a lifetime.

Confused and embarrassed by her strong feelings, Clara watched the water where the marlin disappeared. They must surely think she was crazy by now. Randi would be angry with her for embarrassing her in front of her friends. "I'm sorry," she murmured and rushed below deck. She was leaning against the wall crying when Randi came in.

"Clara, I'm sorry. We were cruel to even consider killing it. That was a dream catch, and we got carried away. Please don't be angry with us," she begged.

Clara turned and was in her arms sobbing.

Randi held her gently. "It's all right," she whispered.

Clara slowly became aware of the heat from Randi's body, and her sobs lessened. Randi's hand gently stroked her hair and neck as her lips lightly brushed Clara's cheek. Clara's arms tightened involuntarily around Randi's waist, pulling her closer. Randi's hands trailed down her neck to her shoulders. Clara gasped when Randi softly kissed her neck. She turned and sought Randi's lips, gently searching. Randi pulled away slightly, questioning.

"No," Clara whispered, her hands took Randi's face and pulled it back to her. Their lips met and Clara felt as if her soul was being devoured. She almost screamed in pleasure when Randi's tongue gently parted her lips. Sliding her hands to Randi's hips, she pulled her tightly against her. Randi leaned back again, and Clara could see her eyes glazed with desire.

After several deep breaths Randi said hoarsely, "Lisa and Rosie are right outside. We'd better stop while we still can."

Clara blushed and hung her head, realizing what she'd just done. "I'm sorry."

"Are you?" Randi asked, placing a finger under her chin and lifting it until she was gazing into her eyes.

Clara felt herself being drawn into those pools of gray. She tried to speak but instead found herself in Randi's arms again, drowning in the warmth of another kiss.

"Randi," Rosie's voice called as she poked her head around the door.

Clara and Randi quickly broke apart, but they were too late.

"Excuse me. I was, I mean, Lisa and I were worried that . . ." She stood staring at her shoes.

Lisa walked in behind her, unaware of what had been going on. "Clara, we're sorry. We just didn't think. You landed that beautiful marlin, and we kind of lost our heads, I guess."

Rosie was pulling her ear. "She landed more than that," she mumbled.

Puzzled, Lisa stared at her while Randi and Clara stood side by side looking uncomfortable. "What's wrong?" Lisa asked.

Rosie took her hand. "Why don't you come and help me turn this tub around? I think they've caught all they want to catch today. If you'll excuse us," she said and pulled a still protesting Lisa back up the stairs.

"Are you all right?" Randi asked.

Clara nodded and smiled.

"I'm sorry she walked in. I'm afraid I wasn't paying much attention."

"I'm glad she came in," Clara confessed, laughing at the surprise on Randi's face. "Now I won't have to sneak into your room in the middle of the night."

Randi smiled and took her into her arms and kissed her gently. "Until tonight."

No one mentioned the incident. At Randi and Clara's insistence, they spent the rest of the day sightseeing and returned to the house only long enough to shower and change before going back out for Chinese food.

Clara was amazed at how rapidly her heart pounded when Randi's leg accidentally pressed against hers when the waitress seated them. She was in such a state that she couldn't remember afterward if the food was good or not.

They returned to the house early. A slight evening chill had settled.

"If you two aren't too tired, I thought we might build a fire and just sit for a while," Rosie said, a slight grin forming at the corners of her lips.

"That's fine," Randi agreed.

Rosie built a small fire while Lisa went for a bottle of wine. Rosie threw several large pillows on the floor in front of the fireplace. After putting on some music, she dimmed the lights.

"All right," Lisa exclaimed when she entered the room and found them sitting on the floor before the fire. "This is my kind of Saturday night." She handed each of them a glass of wine. A slow song began, and she took Rosie's hand. "Let's dance," she said. Walking into the soft shadows, they began to sway slowly to the music.

Randi put her arm around Clara and kissed her gently.

"Randi," she said softly, "I want a divorce."

Leaning back, Randi stared into her eyes. "But darlin', we've just met," she drawled.

"Don't tease me. I want to divorce Allen."

"What about the boys?"

Clara sat staring into the fire. "It's up to them. They're both old enough to make their own decisions. I just know I can't live with him any longer."

"What will you do?"

Until that moment Clara hadn't known what she wanted, but suddenly it was crystal clear. "I'd like to stay with you. I'll start looking for work. There must be something I'm qualified to do." Not waiting for Randi to answer, she rushed on. "I've been unhappy for such a long time, and suddenly I've found something that feels so right."

"I'd like for you to stay," Randi cut in.

Clara felt her heart skip a beat when she looked into Randi's eyes and saw her own desires reflected there. "I want to make love to you," Clara said, cupping Randi's face in her hands. They quietly slipped from the room.

Randi dimmed the light until they were surrounded by soft shadows. She flipped a switch on the wall, and music poured softly over them. Pulling Clara to her, they began to dance.

Clara could smell the sweet scent of Randi's body. She was almost overpowered by the feel of Randi in her arms. Slowly, Randi began to kiss Clara's eyelids, her lips brushing lightly down Clara's cheek to her neck. They stopped dancing and stood gazing at each other.

Clara wanted to memorize every detail of Randi's face. She ran her fingers through Randi's short black hair and down her back. She gasped when Randi's hands slid along the sides of her breasts and sent waves of desire surging through her.

Randi led her to the bed, slowly kissing her neck. Their lips melted together, tongues searching and demanding. She unbuttoned Clara's blouse. Pulling it free, she pushed it off her shoulders. Her hands roamed the length of Clara's back.

Clara felt her bra give under Randi's hand, releasing the full creamy white breasts. She moaned as Randi's lips trailed down her throat to rest between her breasts.

Randi cupped a hand over each of them and kissed them in turn. Her mouth encircled a firm nipple and pulled it slowly into her mouth.

Clara's body grew hotter with Randi's mouth greedily sucking first one and then the other hardening nipple. Her wants grew to be too much. She pushed Randi's hand between her thighs. Never had she felt such desire. She could hear Randi's ragged breathing as Randi pushed her onto the bed and rolled her over on her back.

Randi knelt beside her, running her tongue like a hot iron down her stomach. She worked her way slowly back up to Clara's breasts, where her tongue lingered before moving up to capture her mouth. Randi kissed her hungrily, making promises of things to come.

Clara felt the zipper of her pants slide down under Randi's hand. The pants slipped off her hips. Randi's kisses seared a path along her stomach. Clara caught her breath when Randi's tongue ran along the edge of her thin lace underwear. Gently, Randi kissed the damp cloth between her thighs. Clara urgently grabbed Randi's head, pulling her closer.

Randi's fingers crept deftly under the edge of the material while her mouth continued to work through it. Her fingers glided into the creamy wetness and slid slowly back and forth. With her free hand she pulled the lace barrier aside and softly tongued the silken folds.

Clara felt as though she would die each time Randi pulled away. Finally unable to wait any longer, she cried urgently "Now," and wrapped her legs tightly around Randi's shoulders.

Randi relented and let her fingers glide deep inside while her mouth sucked greedily on the hardened bud.

Clara heard her own raw voice as a wave of pleasure washed over her. A kaleidoscope of colors burst behind her eyes, and each time they began to dim, Randi buried her tongue inside her, causing a new wave to begin.

Just when Clara was certain there could be nothing left, Randi slid alongside her and kissed her passionately. The feel of Randi's demanding tongue and the musky scent of her own pleasure caused a new fire to blaze. She could feel the heavy denim of Randi's jeans against her leg. Desperately she rolled over and spread Randi's legs with her knee. The heavy fold of material over Randi's zipper bit into her, absorbing her wetness. She rocked frantically against Randi until her own body stiffened and arched sharply. Clara's body began to tremble, and she cried out as an orgasm overtook her and sent her soaring to heights she had never dreamed possible.

She lay trembling with exhaustion and tried to speak, but words wouldn't form. She could hear Randi calling from far away. Clara slowly pulled herself from the shroud of bliss that enfolded her.

Randi was gazing down at her smiling. "Are you okay?"

Clara couldn't remember ever seeing anyone look at her with such concern and tenderness. Tears of happiness blinded her. "Randi," she whispered. "Please don't leave me."

"I'm not going anywhere. You rest," she said, gently pulling Clara's head to her shoulder.

Clara's eyes opened slowly. She realized she must have dozed, because she was under the sheet and Randi's naked body lay next to her. The music was still playing softly. Embarrassed at having fallen asleep, she moved slightly to look at the clock by the bedside.

"Hi," Randi whispered, kissing her cheek.

"I'm sorry."

"Shh, you've only been dozing a few minutes. It's better this way," she assured her. "Now that you're rested we can start all over." Randi slid on top of her.

Clara moaned when Randi's naked body molded to hers. "You're so soft," she marveled, running her hand timidly over Randi's back while Randi's hand slowly traveled up her thigh.

"Not this time," Clara whispered, rolling from under her. Shyly she let her lips and fingers explore Randi's body. "I want to know every inch of you," she said, pulling Randi beneath her and lowering her lips to a hard brown nipple. Randi's breasts were small but extremely responsive to Clara's touch. Clara felt herself growing wet again just listening to Randi's moans. She slid slowly down Randi's body and let her tongue and lips explore her hard flat stomach. Her hand inched between Randi's legs. Randi's moan and the wetness she found there filled her with such a strong mixture of power and protectiveness that she had to resist crying out.

Her lips for the first time brushed against the curly mass of Randi's pubic hair. Her nostrils filled with the sweet heady scent of a woman. Clara felt as though she were about to explode from the overload of sensations coursing through her. She gently spread Randi's swollen lips and stared at the glistening jewel before her. Never had she wanted to please a person so much as when her hands reached beneath Randi's hips and lifted her to her lips.

The next morning a soft knock woke them. Stretching, Randi pulled on her robe and went to the door. She returned with a tray bearing a bottle of champagne, orange juice, and a bowl of strawberries. "How's this for room service?" she asked, carefully placing the tray on a table next to the bed. Seeing a card on the tray, Clara picked it up and read it aloud. *Had to leave on some business. See you for lunch — be ready! Rosie and Lisa.*

"That still gives us a couple of hours." Randi smiled wickedly. Picking up a strawberry from the bowl, she offered the end of it to Clara. "Let me show you a new recipe for strawberries," she whispered, gently rubbing the remainder of the strawberry across Clara's hardening nipple.

CHAPTER SIX

It was dark when they arrived back at the beach house Sunday night. Shutting off the motor, Randi pulled Clara close and kissed her deeply. "Just think," she teased, "you don't have to sleep on the couch anymore."

"Let's get in the house before I attack you here in the car," Clara whispered.

"We'll unpack tomorrow," Randi said, jumping out and running toward the house. They burst through the door laughing. Grabbing Randi from behind, Clara buried her face in her neck. "Randi," she sighed, "I love —" The phone rang sharply, shattering the stillness of the night. "Let it ring," Clara moaned.

Laughing, Randi pulled away and answered the phone. "Hello."

Clara watched the smile fade from her face. "It's for you," she said and handed the receiver to Clara. She stood staring at the phone. Only Belinda knew where she was, and she wouldn't call unless something was wrong. Her knees were shaking as she raised the receiver to her ear. She clung to Randi's hand.

"Hello."

"Clara, it's Belinda. I'm sorry but —" her voice broke.

"What's wrong?"

"Roger's been hurt."

Randi was pushing her into a chair. "How bad?"

"A car hit him. He's in intensive care. You'd better come back." Clara dropped the receiver. She was vaguely aware of Randi picking it up and talking and of Randi placing another call. Within minutes of their arrival home, they were on their way back to Corpus. Lisa and Rosie met them at the airport with their tickets. Clara was barely aware of their sympathetic words. Less than an hour later, she and Randi were flying toward Shreveport.

Randi tried several times during the flight to talk to her, but Clara closed her out. She had to prepare herself for facing Allen's anger. When they arrived, thanks to Rosie and Lisa, a rental car was waiting for them. With the aid of a map from the rental agency, Randi drove them to the hospital.

Clara knew she should say something, but she

was afraid if she opened her mouth she would start begging Randi to take her back to Corpus and away from this nightmare. She let Randi lead her through the emergency-room doors and felt herself withdraw further as the medium-built man with the dark curly hair started toward them. She could see the anger in Allen's face. She wanted to send Randi away to protect her from him.

As he grew nearer, Clara sank against a wall, hoping to draw strength from it.

"What are you doing here?" he spat. "It's all your damn fault. You weren't here to take care of him. You've killed him."

She was too late. Her son was dead.

Something sharp stung Clara's nostrils. She opened her eyes to find Randi and a nurse hovering over her. She was lying on a table in an examining room. She tried to sit up, but Randi pushed her back gently. "Lie still. You're okay."

"I want to see Roger. Where is he?" She breathed a sigh of relief that Allen was not in sight.

"Can she see him?" Randi asked the nurse. Clara clung to Randi's hand tightly.

"Not for a while. He's still in surgery," the nurse said, checking Clara's blood pressure. Both Randi and Clara turned to her.

"Surgery." Clara fought her way up again.

"I thought he was . . ." Randi trailed off.

"He's still alive?" Clara's heart pounded wildly. Hadn't Allen said he was dead, or had she just misunderstood him?

"I'm sorry, but you'll have to talk to the doctor." The nurse looked at her watch before adding, "He should be out shortly. Now you just lie back and rest. I'll come and get you as soon as the doctor is available." With a smile and light pat on Clara's arm, she left.

Clara slid off the table and leaned against it. Randi held out an arm to steady her. "Randi, I'm so scared." She began to sob.

"I know you are. It's going to be okay." She took her into her arms and gently kissed her.

"What the hell is going on in here?" Allen stood in the doorway glaring at them.

Clara pulled away and stared at him. Was it her imagination or did he seem smaller, less intimidating? Or was it because Randi was here beside her? She squared her shoulders, determined not to let him bully her. "What's happened to Roger?"

"Who are you?" he roared, ignoring Clara's question and glaring at Randi, his face purple with rage. "Why were you kissing my wife?" He stalked toward them.

Randi started to speak, but Clara stopped her by placing a hand on her arm. "Allen, I asked you about Roger. How is he?"

He pushed by Randi and grabbed Clara's shoulders. He seemed to see her short hair for the first time. "What have you done to your hair?" He looked down at her clothes. "You're wearing pants. You look like a damn dyke." He shook her. "Where have you been?" Clara felt her newfound confidence slipping.

Randi stepped forward. "She's been with me."

73

He whirled back around. "Who the hell are you?"

Clara felt the anger spark through the room as Randi and Allen stood facing each other.

In a voice that was eerily calm, Randi replied, "I'm her lover."

Frightened, Clara stepped between them. She had never seen Allen so angry. He was glaring at Randi, and Randi was meeting his glare with no sign of backing down. For one terrible moment Clara was afraid he would actually strike Randi. When his anger failed to intimidate Randi, he turned it on Clara. "You were with this dyke doing God-knows-what while our son was being killed?"

"He's not dead," she snapped.

"It's all your fault. God is punishing you for your sins by hurting my son." He looked at each of them and sneered. "You should be locked away from decent people."

For a moment Allen sounded so much like her strict fundamentalist father that Clara had to remind herself that she wasn't a child anymore. In the face of his growing anger, Clara felt her courage slip more.

"Leave her alone," Randi said sharply. "If God's punishing anyone, it's you for your cruelty."

Clara watched helplessly as Allen and Randi continued to tear at each other. The noise and the walls began closing in again. Her son could be dying, and no one seemed to care. She pressed her hands over her ears and screamed, "Shut up."

Startled, they both turned to stare at her. "Please," she sobbed.

Randi's face reddened. "I'm sorry," she murmured.

Allen stared at the two of them. Turning to Randi he snarled, "Get out of here. I'd like to be alone with my *wife*."

"I'm not going anywhere," Randi snapped and glowered back at him.

"Perhaps we should let Clara decide." He turned his attention back to Clara. "Are you staying here with me or do you want a divorce to live with your," he threw a look of contempt toward Randi, "*lover*?" Sure of himself, he put his hands in his pockets and smiled. "You should think about a few things before you decide. If you leave or file for a divorce, I'll tell everyone about your friend here, and you'll never see either of the boys again. Not that they'd want to see you anyway after they hear why you left them."

Clara felt as though the blood had been drained from her body. If he hated her so much, why wouldn't he just go away and leave her alone?

"Tell her to get out," he persisted.

Clara stared at him before lowering her head. She could feel Randi watching her. Clara wanted to say something but couldn't. She knew Allen. He wouldn't let up until he had destroyed them both. He'd tell the boys. How would they react? Would they hate her? She could simply leave with Randi now, but what would he do then? She already knew the answer to that. He'd never stop hounding them. She knew Randi was waiting for her to say something.

Suddenly Randi whirled around and headed toward the door. Clara started to reach for her but stopped. If Allen knew how much Randi meant to her, he would not quit until he destroyed Randi.

"Wait," Allen commanded. Randi and Clara both

stared at him. He was looking at Clara with a sick smile. "I want you to tell her to leave. I don't want her to ever doubt who threw her out of here."

"Allen, I'm here. Isn't that enough?" she pleaded.

"No." His eyes held hers. She shivered at the insane glint.

"I won't ask for a divorce." Her voice shook with sobs.

He leaned toward her, beads of perspiration standing out on his forehead. His eyes were glazed over with hatred. "Tell her."

"Allen, you're sick," she said in a voice hardly more than a whisper.

He slapped her hard. Randi started across the floor, but Clara held out her hand to stop her. For the first time since entering the hospital, Clara looked in Randi's eyes. Being with Randi had been the best three weeks of her life. She would never forget Randi's kisses and gentle caresses, but Allen would do everything he threatened. He wouldn't rest until he had destroyed them. Clara loved Randi too much to put her through that. She needed time to think. But they were both waiting for her to speak. Taking a deep breath, she did the only thing she felt she could do at the moment, and she prayed that Randi would understand.

"Randi, please leave," she whispered.

Pain filled Randi's eyes. Clara watched, alarmed, as the pain burned away, and her soft gray eyes turned a cold steel gray. Randi stormed from the room and Clara felt a large part of herself die when she realized that Randi might not ever want her back.

Allen walked toward her. His hand turned her

face toward him. "Starting tonight," he rasped, "you're going to be my wife again."

Looking up at him, she was consumed with hatred. Randi was gone. "Go to hell," she seethed.

He raised his hand to strike her again, but Clara drew her shoulders back and met his gaze with a glare.

"If you ever hit me again, I'll kill you. I swear," she hissed. Allen's eyes widened as he slowly backed up and left the room.

Thirty minutes later, a short, slightly overweight doctor approached Clara.

"Mrs. Webster, I'm Dr. Fellows. Your son has been taken to recovery." He sat in the chair next to her.

"How is he?" Clara asked, clutching her arms tightly against her stomach.

"When he was brought in he was hemorrhaging, and we had to remove his spleen. He's stabilized now, but we'll be keeping a close watch on him for the next few hours." He patted her arm. "Your son is going to be fine. It'll just take some time."

"When can I see him?"

"You'll be allowed to see him for five minutes every hour on the hour. He needs his rest."

Clara thanked him and settled back to wait. Allen returned just before it was time to go in to see Roger.

"We should pretend that nothing's happened for his sake," Allen said, sitting in the chair beside her.

"I'm through pretending, and I'm through with you," she said, moving as far away from him as the chair would allow.

A nurse approached them. "You can go in now."

When Clara saw her son lying in the sterile white

bed, she felt a large fist close around her heart. He looked so young and innocent. Tears blurred her vision.

"Roger," she whispered. He opened his dark eyes and stared at her. She saw recognition flicker in his expression and she smiled. "How do you feel?" she asked, brushing the dark hair away from his forehead. He continued to stare.

"Mom, where have you been?"

"I had to leave for a while." She wiped away her tears. "We'll talk about it after you're feeling better."

"Why do you look like that?" he asked weakly.

"Like what, sugar?"

"Your hair. You cut it."

"That's the way dykes wear their hair, son." Allen smiled maliciously at Clara.

Clara was so dumbfounded by his statement that for a moment she could only look at him. Roger was watching her, as if waiting for her to say something.

"That's why you got hurt," Allen said. "She wasn't here taking care of you the way she should've been." He took Roger's hand. "She was out running around with her girlfriend."

"Allen, for god's sake," Clara sputtered.

"I thought you were through pretending," Allen challenged. "Tell the boy I'm lying."

Clara felt an anger unequal to any she had ever experienced. She suddenly knew the full meaning of the term *murderous rage*.

"Mom," Roger whispered. "That ain't true, is it?"

"Of course not," Clara started, but stopped. She wasn't going to allow Allen to rule her life any longer. She took Roger's other hand, careful not to disturb the IV tubes. "I never left you for anyone. I needed time alone."

"But you certainly didn't spend it alone, did you?" Allen persisted.

Clara glared at him and wished fervently that he would simply disappear. "Allen, this is neither the time nor the place."

"Go ahead. Explain to him about your new dyke *lover*. He's old enough to know the truth. You keep babying him, and he'll grow up to be a fag. Or is that what you want?"

Clara saw the look of shock on Roger's face. "Allen, this is between you and me. Leave him out of it."

"You ain't no dyke are you, Mom?"

Clara met the dark eyes so much like her own and took a deep breath. She wasn't going to lie. "Yes, Roger. I was involved with a woman, but that's over with now. I'm home."

"Of course, it's only a matter of time before she goes running off with another one," Allen said, staring at Clara.

"Don't judge me by your standards," she snapped. "Roger, your father's wrong."

Roger seemed to think for a minute as his gaze wandered to each of them. His eyes suddenly blazed, and he turned on Clara. "Dad's never wrong," he defended. "He stayed with us and didn't run off with some dyke and leave us like you did." He was becoming agitated.

Clara felt her knees buckle. Catching herself, she sat weakly on the side of his bed. "That's not what happened."

"You don't love us no more."

"Roger, that isn't true. I'll always love you and Jamie. Nothing could ever change that. No matter what else happens, you have to believe me."

"No, I hate you. I never want to see you again. And I'm going to tell Jamie so he won't want to see you either."

"Roger, no," she sobbed. "Please let me explain."

"No. You'll just find someone else and leave again. I'm going to tell everyone you're queer so you can't ever come back."

Clara recoiled from the hatred that poured from her son. She couldn't meet Allen's gaze. A nurse was at her side leading her out and talking to her, but Clara couldn't understand what she was saying. Roger's glare followed her to the door. Unable to face the hatred in his eyes, she ran from the hospital and continued to run through the darkness until her sides ached. Finding herself by a phone booth, she dialed Belinda's number. She answered on the first ring.

"Clara, I've been worried sick about you. I was going to go to the hospital, but I was afraid to leave the house thinking you might call. Are you at the hospital?"

"No," she whispered.

"What's wrong?"

"Can you come and get me?" she sobbed.

"Oh dear God, he isn't . . ."

"No, Roger will be fine. I'm at the corner of . . ." She glanced around for a street sign. "Beaker and Appleton. Please come and get me."

"I'll be there in fifteen minutes. You just stay where you are."

Clara collapsed on a bench by a bus stop. Allen had tricked her and caused her to lose Randi. No, she told herself. She had lost Randi all by herself due to her own foolishness. In the few weeks she had known Randi she had grown to love her deeply. She remembered the hatred in Randi's eyes and shuddered. Roger's and Allen's eyes had looked the same way. Everyone hated her. Why did the people she tried hardest to love hate her? She continued to chase the elusive answers to her questions until Belinda's face floated before her.

"Clara, are you all right? Come on and get in the car. This isn't the greatest neighborhood at three in the morning."

"Three," she whispered. "Belinda, I'm sorry. I didn't realize it was so late." Sobs once again choked her.

"Come on. Get in. I'll help you." A few minutes later they sat in Belinda's tiny apartment. Clara was holding a glass of brandy. "Drink it," Belinda told her. "Then tell me what's going on."

Clara was petrified. How could she tell her last friend in the world about Randi? Would she hate her too? She downed the brandy in two gulps. The liquor burned her throat and chest, causing her to cough harshly. Belinda refilled her glass, and once more Clara drained it. This time it didn't burn as bad.

Belinda looked at her closely. "I'm not going to refill that glass until you tell me what's going on."

Clara took a deep breath. She could already feel the liquor's warm sensations coursing through her veins. "Maybe you'd better have one too." Clara motioned toward the bottle.

Belinda took her glass and poured herself a drink, downed it, and sat back. "All right. We should be properly fortified. Now, let's hear it."

Taking another deep breath, she stood and began to pace. Seeing a pack of cigarettes on the table, Clara took one and lit it. She remembered how Randi had gotten into the habit of lighting two and handing her one. Tears sprang into her eyes and rolled slowly down her cheeks. Clara returned to the slightly battered couch and sat next to her.

"When I left here," she began, "I just started driving, going nowhere in particular. I stopped on a beach and sat staring out at the water. I decided I was too tired to go on living." Belinda took her hand and squeezed. "I walked out into the water with every intention of drowning myself."

"Jesus, Clara," Belinda whispered. "Why?"

Clara shook her head to stop her. She had to finish before she lost her nerve. "I almost did it, but a woman tried to pull me out, and in the process I nearly drowned her instead." Clara shrugged slightly. "I ended up pulling her out. Anyway, she took me home with her. For the first time in twenty years, I felt like a normal intelligent human. We had conversa- tions and laughed. I discovered I wasn't as dull and stupid as Allen always said."

"I told you that." The hurt in Belinda's voice was obvious.

Sensing her friend's pain, Clara gently squeezed her hand. "I know you tried, but I guess I never really listened because you were a friend. You always loved me no matter what. Randi was a stranger.

82

Someone who had no prior knowledge of me and still liked me."

After a brief pause, Belinda nodded. "I think I understand."

"She saved my life, Belinda. Not by simply stopping me from drowning, but by making me feel alive." Clara hesitated and removed her hand from Belinda's and faced her. "I fell in love with her," she said in a barely audible voice. Clara watched the blood drain from Belinda's face. *She'll hate me too*, she thought. After a pause, Belinda poured herself another drink with trembling hands. The liquor sloshed over her fingers as she tried to drink.

"I'm sorry I've upset you," Clara said. "Perhaps it would be best if I left."

"No," Belinda cried. "Clara, I'm sorry. It's just surprised me, that's all." Taking a deep breath, she lit a cigarette. "Give me a minute, because we really need to talk. But first, finish your story."

Clara told her about the weekend she and Randi had spent in Corpus, and how Allen had reacted when she returned.

"What are you going to do now?" Belinda asked after Clara had finished her story.

"I don't know."

"Do you plan on going back to Randi?" she asked slowly.

"It's too late. She hates me for being weak and sending her away."

"It could be your imagination. Besides, if Allen's already told the boys, what do you have to lose?"

"Randi's career. She's a respected artist," Clara said.

"Don't you think you should at least ask her opinion of whether it would affect her career or not?" Belinda asked, reaching over and squeezing Clara's trembling hand.

"No. She wouldn't think about herself."

"The arts are a pretty liberal field, Clara. I doubt if Allen's outing her would hurt her very much."

"It's not just him telling everyone about her. It's the emotional shit he'd put us through. He wouldn't give up until she was destroyed."

"What are you going to do?" Belinda asked.

"As soon as Roger's well, I'm going to leave. I don't need a divorce from Allen. He can ask for one if he wants to. I'll find a job and make a life for myself." She hesitated. "Are we still friends?"

Belinda stared into her empty glass. "We'll always be friends." She put out her cigarette. "There's something I've wanted to tell you for some time now, but never had the courage." She looked at Clara and took another deep breath. "In college there was this girl. We were roommates my sophomore year. We got to be good friends. I thought she was the warmest, funniest person I'd ever met. One night we got a little stoned and she kissed me. We became lovers. We were accidentally discovered and expelled." Clara took her hand again as Belinda rushed on. "I was so ashamed of people thinking I was a lesbian that two weeks after I got home I married James to stop any rumors and remove all doubt. We were married barely a year before our divorce. I never loved him, and I cringed every time he touched me."

She turned the glass around slowly in her hand. "A while later I met Ray. He was gentle and understanding, almost like a woman, but not quite." She well. Just before he was due to be released, she tried to call him. He hung up when he heard her voice. She had tried calling Jamie numerous times at home, but either no one answered or Allen answered and told her Jamie didn't want to speak to her.

She finally gathered enough courage to borrow Belinda's car and go back to the house to pick up the rest of her clothes. She had been borrowing clothes from Belinda, but Belinda's slightly smaller frame meant the clothes were tight and uncomfortable. When she got to the house, Clara was shocked to find her station wagon sitting in the driveway. Apparently, Randi had driven it back. For one wild moment she imagined Randi was in the house waiting for her. Rushing up the steps, she tried to unlock the door, but the key no longer fit. Allen had changed the locks. Luckily, her suitcase and the clothes that she and Randi had picked out in Corpus were in the station wagon. As she was transferring everything to Belinda's car, she found the painting of the birds that Randi had wanted to throw away. For a brief moment she could hear the waves crashing and smell the salty air. Clutching the painting to her, she sat on the porch to wait until Jamie came home from school. He saw her and quickly walked on by the house.

"Jamie, wait. I want to talk to you," she called.

He started running. Clara forced herself to breathe as she got into Belinda's car and drove away. It was obvious neither of the boys wanted her in their lives anymore. That evening she sat on the couch and cried herself to sleep in Belinda's arms.

sighed softly. "I divorced him too. I was still lying to myself. I couldn't be a lesbian, so I married Mark. You remember him. He was all man. The no-shit-from-no-woman kind. I had this archaic notion he would make a *real* woman out of me. He tried for six months before he kicked me out. The only good thing that came from my marriage to Mark was that I finally admitted to myself that I was a lesbian." She pulled her hand free, ran it across her finely chiseled face, and breathed a hollow laugh. "I just didn't know what to do about it."

They sat in silence for a moment as Belinda seemed to gather her thoughts. "A few months later, I accidentally picked up a gay newsletter that someone had left on the bus." Belinda tapped the ash from her cigarette. "When I first picked it up and started thumbing through it, I didn't pay much attention to what I was seeing. But when I realized what I had, I almost died of embarrassment and hid it in my purse. After I got home, I read it from cover to cover until I practically wore it out." She stretched her long legs under the coffee table.

"I wanted to subscribe to the paper, but I was so paranoid that everyone would find out that I was a lesbian. Finally, I went downtown and got a post office box. *Then* I subscribed to the paper. I started getting every lesbian newsletter and magazine I could find. In some of them were letters from women who had gone or were going through the same thing I was. I started writing to these women through these publications, and you know what?" She turned to Clara. "I discovered I wasn't ashamed any longer. That I was proud to be a lesbian. I've recently begun speaking out publicly. Those trips I'm always running off on are usually workshops or a seminar that I'm speaking at." She looked into Clara's eyes. "So you see," she said softly, "you haven't offended me in the least."

Clara was dumbfounded. How could she have not known? Belinda had been her closest friend, her only friend, she amended, for over seven years. Stricken with guilt, she shook her head. "All those years I spent crying on your shoulder, you were trying to get your life together. I'm so sorry I wasn't there for you. You never once complained, and it must have been hell to go through it alone." She took Belinda's hand again.

"Once I accepted who I was, I wasn't alone. I had an entire network of women writing and calling, pulling for me every step of the way," she said and wiped a tear from Clara's cheek. "Call Randi. Talk to her."

Clara shook her head. "I can't. I have to see if I can make a life for myself first. Then maybe I can make a life with someone else."

CHAPTER SEVEN

It was decided that Clara would be living at Belinda's until Roger was better or until she could afford to move. They were cramped in the small one-bedroom apartment, and Clara once again found herself sleeping on the couch. There were days when after fruitlessly searching the want ads she questioned her ability to compete in the business world, but she never doubted her decision to leave Allen. Clara hadn't been able to make herself return to the hospital, but she called the nurse's station twice a day to check on Roger's progress. He was healing

* * * * *

Clara filled her days looking for work and reading the lesbian publications that were scattered around Belinda's apartment. Her lack of job skills and work experience seriously limited her choices for employment, but she kept looking. Belinda had gradually convinced her to try writing articles for some of the publications she had been reading. Clara spent hours in the library poring over books on journalism trying to sharpen her writing skills.

A few weeks after Clara moved in, Belinda insisted Clara needed to get out and meet people and took her to a meeting of the local lesbian task force. Clara fell in love with the group and threw herself into it with an almost frantic determination. She was soon in charge of their monthly publication, the *Rag*. Due to overworked or less-than-eager volunteers, subscriptions to the paper were low. Clara knew that the low rate could be attributed to the paper's sporadic publishing schedule and its outdated articles. It barely paid for itself. Clara set out with a vengeance to turn the paper around.

As the weeks slipped by, she struggled to remain optimistic and kept submitting articles until at long last one was accepted for publication and she was hooked once more on journalism. A week later, she found a part-time job working at a small weekly newspaper. She helped set up ads and retype copy. The pay was horrible, but at least she had gotten her foot in the door, and the hours gave her plenty of time to concentrate on her writing. On those rare occasions when everything threatened to overwhelm her, Belinda encouraged her along. Clara began to feel that at long last her life was beginning to take shape.

A month later she was served with divorce papers. Allen called that same night and threatened to make things nasty for her if she contested. Clara called Diana Green, a lawyer she had met on the task force. Diana arranged for a meeting with Allen and his lawyer. It was decided that Clara would not contest the divorce and that Allen would give her a lump sum payment of half the value of the house and the savings account. Allen insisted they sign an agreement to never make further monetary demands of the other. The only painful thing for Clara was that the boys wanted to live with their father. Diana told her she would get more if she held out, but Clara didn't want to deal with him any longer than absolutely necessary. She was in a hurry to get on with her life.

After leaving Allen's lawyer's office, Clara and Diana stopped for lunch.

"You know, you let him off too easy," Diana said, pulling the radishes from her salad.

"Maybe, but I just want out," Clara admitted, picking at her sandwich.

"Let's hope you still feel that way a year from now. It's hard for a single woman with no previous work experience to survive financially with today's economy."

"Belinda says I can stay with her until I get on

my feet, but I'm eager to get out on my own." Clara pushed the sandwich away. The day's events had left her without an appetite. "When the settlement check arrives, I'm going to start looking for a place."

"Where will you be looking? I might be able to help you find something."

Clara had a brief longing for the Texas coast but pushed the thought away. "Maybe here in Shreveport, or I may decide to leave Louisiana completely and start over fresh somewhere."

Diana looked up quickly. "Leave Shreveport. Why? We've really come to depend on you at the task force. Everyone I talk to is raving about the improvements you've made to the *Rag*," she said, referring to the task force's ailing paper. "I hear it's actually beginning to show a small profit."

Clara smiled, warmed by her praise. "Thanks, but the *Rag* is only six pages. That doesn't take a lot of effort. It just needed someone to spend some time on it."

"You know," Diana replied, "it was originally planned for statewide distribution as a means of letting Louisiana lesbians know what was going on, but we just never found anyone who was willing to put in the effort to develop it. Would you be interested in trying to expand it?"

Clara's interest was piqued. "Would that still be an option?"

Diana shrugged. "I know that money was set aside for the paper. Why don't we bring it up at the next meeting?"

Clara's mind began to sift through ideas for the paper. As she did so, she reached for her sandwich again and began to eat. She laughed when she looked up to find Diana smiling at her. "Maybe I will stay in Shreveport," she said with a nod.

At the next meeting Clara received an enthusiastic go-ahead to expand the *Rag*'s format.

On a hot, steamy afternoon in July, Clara came home from work to find Belinda waiting for her with two glasses and a bottle of champagne.

"Happy birthday," she said with a smile and handed Clara a glass.

Clara kicked off her shoes and dug her toes into the cool, tan carpet. "Thank you." She held the glasses as Belinda poured the champagne. They both sat on the couch and sipped their drinks.

"You've never forgotten my birthday," Clara said when Belinda handed her a small box. "I can't tell you how much you've helped me during these last two months. I can't ever thank you enough." Clara was discouraged. She was having problems finding an apartment. When she found something she liked and could afford, Belinda came up with a dozen excuses as to why it was all wrong. Clara, however, was determined to keep looking.

"I didn't do it for you to thank me. Now open the box," Belinda scolded softly.

Clara set her glass down and stripped away the paper. Inside the box was a thin, gold chain. "It's beautiful," she exclaimed, holding it up. "You shouldn't have done this. You've already done so much."

"Stop fussing. Here, let me help you." Belinda

leaned over and placed her glass next to Clara's before fastening the necklace. Clara's skin tingled where Belinda's fingers touched her neck.

Clara turned and hugged her and was shocked at the wave of desire that washed over her. Surprised, she pulled away and busied herself folding the ragged scraps of wrapping paper. She had never thought of Belinda as anything but a friend.

Belinda placed her hand on Clara's arm. "What do I have to do to get you to stop running from me?" Her voice was low, hardly more than a whisper.

Clara looked up and found she was unable to turn away from the raw hunger in Belinda's gaze.

"You have green eyes," she said suddenly, reaching out to caress Belinda's cheek. "Why haven't I noticed before?"

"You've been too busy running from me," Belinda murmured, rubbing her cheek against Clara's hand.

Clara's breath caught as a flame of need shot through her. It had been so long since Randi. She pushed the thought away and leaned forward to kiss Belinda's forehead. Belinda gave a soft groan when Clara's lips brushed lightly against her eyelids and moved slowly down until their lips met. Clara's tongue slipped between Belinda's lips.

"I want you," Belinda whispered, unbuttoning Clara's blouse. "I've dreamed of this so many times." She pulled away. "I want to see you. Take your clothes off."

Belinda watched Clara unbutton her blouse and remove it.

Belinda's devouring eyes made Clara feel beautiful. She unfastened her bra and let it fall away. She heard the sharp intake of breath and saw the desire in Belinda's eyes. Clara stood and unfastened the belt to her slacks and lowered the zipper.

"Turn around." Belinda's voice was thick with passion.

Clara turned and lowered her slacks and panties down her thighs. Belinda's eyes were on her as she bent to remove the clothing from her ankles.

Belinda's hands ran along Clara's hips. Clara closed her eyes, feeling rather self-conscious about her bent-over position, but found it strangely exciting. Belinda trailed one hand down Clara's tailbone. Clara gasped and stiffened as Belinda's fingers pushed lightly between her cheeks.

"Relax, baby," Belinda cooed, standing behind her and bringing her free hand around to stroke Clara's rock-hard nipples. Clara started to rise.

"No, stay like that," Belinda demanded, pushing Clara's feet apart. "Spread your legs." Clara found herself growing more aroused as she obeyed. "Farther," Belinda insisted, lowering herself behind her. Clara's knees almost folded when Belinda's hands moved back to spread Clara's cheeks and her tongue slowly slid between them. Belinda's tongue continued to delicately stroke as she inserted first two fingers and then four into Clara's wetness. Clara was having trouble standing until Belinda finally stood and slipped an arm around her.

"Just relax. I've got you." Clara moaned loudly when Belinda's fingers inside her became more insistent. "I've got you," Belinda said again. "Spread your legs."

Clara braced her arms against the table in front of her. On the next thrust Clara felt Belinda's hand slide inside. Clara cried out as intense pleasure shot through her. She pushed back onto the hand that Belinda gently thrust into her. Clara's muscles clamped around Belinda's hand, trying to keep it inside her. Belinda was talking to her, but Clara couldn't hear her over the roar of her own rushing blood. Clara's body tensed only seconds before she came so hard she felt wetness running down her thighs.

When Clara could again breathe normally, she realized she was sitting on Belinda's lap on the couch and that Belinda was gently caressing her breasts. "You're a very hot woman," she murmured thickly. "I always knew you would be."

Clara kissed her deeply. Belinda oozed a raw sexuality Clara had never known before. She felt slightly intimidated, but she wanted to please this woman. "Tell me what you want," she whispered, running her tongue along her ear.

"I want you to undress me."

Clara turned and straddled Belinda's legs. She could smell her own musky scent and knew from the smoldering look in Belinda's eyes that she was smelling it also. She pulled the knit top off over Belinda's head and ran her tongue over Belinda's full, dark-pink nipples. Clara lowered herself to the floor between Belinda's legs and tugged off the shorts she was wearing. Belinda slid her hips to the edge of the couch. Clara smiled and lowered her head between the damp, deeply-tanned thighs. Belinda hooked her feet on the legs of the table behind Clara and pushed herself against Clara's eager tongue. Belinda locked her hands behind Clara's head and increased the grinding motion of her hips to a frenzied pace. Clara continued licking the swollen lips long after Belinda had collapsed. She couldn't get enough of her sweet wetness, and she almost shouted with joy when she felt Belinda begin to respond again. Clara pushed the table away and stretched out on the floor. She pulled Belinda down so that Belinda's knees straddled her head. Clara reached up to stroke Belinda's ample breasts. Belinda looked deep into her eyes and gently lifted Clara's head to her throbbing center.

A small Christmas tree twinkled softly as Clara sat on the couch surrounded by Christmas cards, an address book, and a roll of stamps. Balanced on a notebook on her lap was an envelope addressed to Randi and another one addressed to Lisa and Rosie. In Randi's card she had included a letter apologizing for the night at the hospital. The short note had taken her hours to write, and she was still uncertain whether to mail it or not. Lisa and Rosie's had been almost as difficult. She thanked them for their help on that horrible night and reimbursed them for the cost of the two airline tickets. She knew she was extremely tardy in writing the two letters, but she had been unable to do so before. She wanted to apologize to everyone for causing the disruption in their lives, but somehow she couldn't find the words to do so. She was sure they all despised her. And Lisa had pointedly told her she didn't want to see Randi get hurt. Clara agonized for hours over whether to include a return address and finally decided against it, knowing they wouldn't care where she was.

Hearing Belinda's key in the door, Clara hastily pushed the two cards inside the binder and picked up another card and began addressing it to Jamie and Roger. She didn't know what to buy them, so she was sending them money. She hadn't seen or talked to them since the divorce. *Coward*, a small voice inside her called out. Belinda's entrance gave her a temporary reprieve from having to decide what to say to them.

"Hi," Belinda breathed, leaning over to kiss Clara. "How was your day?"

"I worked on the *Rag* most of the day, but I managed to finish that article on breast-cancer funding, and I've started my Christmas cards." Clara had already sold the article to *Wimmin's Room*, a paper out of San Antonio. She wondered briefly if Randi would ever see her byline.

"That's great." Belinda hung up her jacket and placed a shopping bag under their small Christmas tree.

"What's that?" Clara asked, clearing a space for Belinda to sit beside her.

"Oh, just a little something for the love of my life." She smiled and slid to the floor to sit with her back propped against the couch.

Clara rubbed Belinda's head lovingly. "You've already bought too much."

"Never. Come down here and join me." Belinda reached back for her.

Clara moved down, and Belinda guided her

between her outstretched legs so that Clara's back was against her. "I missed you today," Belinda murmured, reaching her arms around Clara and pulling her closer as her lips traveled along Clara's neck. "So what's all this mess around us?" she asked, pushing away a box of Christmas cards.

"I'm trying to finish my Christmas cards. I can't believe I'm so far behind."

Belinda rested her chin on Clara's shoulder. "Are you going to try to see Jamie and Roger during the holidays?

Clara hesitated a second. "No. I don't think they're ready for that yet."

"What makes you say that?"

Clara shrugged.

"Are you sure it's not your own guilt?" Belinda asked.

Clara stiffened, and Belinda held her tighter. "I'm just worried about you," she reassured her.

"I don't think I've ever felt guilty about being a lesbian," Clara stated slowly. "I just wish I had figured it out sooner. I could have saved everyone a lot of pain."

"We all progress at different speeds. Stop beating yourself up over it."

Clara rubbed Belinda's long legs that were stretched out on either side of her. "Why didn't you just bang me on the head years ago and wake me up?" she teased.

Belinda gave a mock shudder. "You were too straight."

"Do you miss spending time with your family?" Clara asked. Her tone was serious. Belinda had come out to her parents and her brother over a year ago, and they were all having trouble handling the news. She hadn't spoken to them since.

Belinda sighed. "Sometimes I miss them, especially my mom, but most of the time I simply feel angry. I'm not any different now than I ever was. That's not true," she suddenly corrected. "I'm happy now. I was never happy when I was married, and they all supported me through my marriages." She rubbed her cheek along Clara's shoulder. "I'm angry that they seem to prefer me unhappy."

"It'll work out," Clara assured her. They fell silent, and Clara gazed at the brightly-lit Christmas tree. Would Randi have a tree? Did she celebrate Christmas? Was she alone?

"Where do you want to be ten years from now?" Clara asked, tearing her thoughts away from Randi.

"Right here." Belinda nuzzled her neck again.

"I'm serious."

"I don't know. I guess I would like to be a successful speaker. I want to do something that will make a difference to our community."

"Do you think we'll still be together?" Clara felt Belinda's body tense slightly.

"You're not going to dump me at Christmas time are you?" Belinda asked with a tight laugh.

"And miss all those great presents over there?"

"Clara, you're a horrible materialistic capitalist, but I do love you."

Clara turned her face back to Belinda. "Show me," she breathed in a provocative whisper.

Belinda's mouth captured hers and claimed it. Belinda was a much more aggressive lover than Randi had been. Clara stopped making comparisons when Belinda's hands made their way under her sweater and began to stroke her breasts. "I love holding you like this," she whispered. "I have total access to your body this way."

"Um," Clara moaned as Belinda cast aside Clara's sweater and ran her lips along her bare shoulders.

Clara hadn't missed the fact that Belinda had avoided the question of their future together, but she soon forgot about it as Belinda's hands slid down into Clara's jeans.

The next day Clara stood in front of the mailbox for ten long agonizing minutes before she finally dropped the cards to Randi and Rosie and Lisa in. The second they left her hands, she regretted her decision. It would have been best just to disappear from Randi's life totally.

By the New Year, Clara's life had fallen into a comfortable routine. She had stopped working at the weekly newspaper because she could now make more money with her articles. She spent many hours working on the *Rag,* which was slowly making its presence known throughout the state. Writing occupied her days and Belinda her nights. She loved Belinda, but no matter how hard she tried, she couldn't forget Randi.

She was laboring over the outline of an article for the *Rag* when Belinda came home early from work. Clara heard the door but wanted to work a while longer before stopping for the day.

"Hello," Belinda purred, kissing her neck.

Clara stopped and turned toward her. "You're home early. Is everything all right?"

"As a matter of fact, things have never been better." She pulled Clara up to face her. "I just received an offer to speak to the Women's Coalition for Justice at the University of New Orleans in April. How would you like to go with me?"

"That's great." Clara knew how important public speaking was to her.

"Will you go with me?" She was grinning wildly.

"Just try keeping me away," Clara said as Belinda's hands slowly worked their way up her thigh. She knew she wouldn't be getting any more work done tonight.

Belinda threw herself into preparing her speech, and Clara helped her rehearse it endlessly, but still on the day she was to speak, Belinda was a nervous wreck.

"This could be my break," she said. They were backstage, and Belinda was pacing nervously.

"You'll be fine," Clara assured her. "I have to go get a seat, but remember I'll be rooting for you. Good luck." She kissed her quickly and left.

Belinda was great, just as Clara had predicted. By the end of her speech she had the audience's complete attention. Thunderous applause broke loose as she stepped from the podium.

Clara hurried backstage to find Belinda already surrounded by a dozen women. Standing to one side, she basked in Belinda's well-earned praise. She saw

Belinda looking for her and waved. Quickly Belinda excused herself and pushed through the crowd toward her.

"What did you think?" she asked nervously.

"Absolutely great, as always." Clara smiled, surrendering to Belinda's giddy kiss.

"We've been invited to a reception. Do you want to go?"

Clara could see the eager anticipation in Belinda's eyes. "Of course."

"Great. Come on, I have to get my stuff."

The reception was already in full swing when they arrived. It looked to Clara as if half the city of New Orleans was there. It wasn't long until they found themselves separated.

Clara was trying to make her way to a less crowded area when a hand reached out and touched her arm.

"Clara Webster?" a young woman with short, spiked, blond hair asked. Puzzled, Clara nodded and stared at her as people continued to jostle around them.

"Let's get out of this crowd before we're trampled," the woman said, taking Clara by the arm and leading her to a fairly quiet corner. "I'm Stacey Benson," she said, extending her hand. "I'm the editor of *Women Who Are*."

Clara recognized the name immediately. The magazine had published several of her articles. "Your magazine has been very kind to me," she said, finding herself staring into Stacey's soft brown eyes.

"Kind!" Stacey echoed. "You're one hell of a writer."

Embarrassed, Clara studied the glass of mineral water she was holding.

Stacey rushed on. "Listen, I want to talk to you about an idea I've had. I was going to call you later in the month, but this has worked out perfect."

"Call me?" Clara frowned and wondered why this woman would be calling her.

"I'm here as the wrap-up speaker for the conference tomorrow, and on my way down I stopped in Shreveport to visit an old friend, Diana Green. I mentioned to her that I was looking for a new editor, and she couldn't stop talking about what you've done with the task force's paper." Stacey raced on, not giving Clara a chance to interrupt. "She told me that you and Belinda Edwards are lovers and that Belinda was speaking tonight. So I came down a day early hoping I'd get a chance to talk to you."

Clara frowned. Diana Green was the lawyer from the task force who helped with her divorce. Since then Clara hadn't seen her except at task force meetings. "You came here to see me? Why?"

"I want to start another magazine on the West Coast. Actually, it's already in existence, but it's failing fast. It's a good magazine, but it needs someone to run it. I can't very well handle both of them. Besides, I don't really want to leave New York," she admitted.

"What's that got to do with me?"

"I'd like for you to be the editor."

Clara stared at her, dumbfounded. "I don't know anything about running a magazine."

"I think you're wrong. I've kept a close eye on

your work. And Diana couldn't stop talking about what a great job you've done with the *Rag*. You may not have all the actual experience necessary, but my instincts tell me you're exactly the fresh blood this magazine needs." Stacey moved them deeper into the corner as someone jostled against them. "Clara," she began, "I can find a dozen qualified editors. But I want a new outlook, and I think you have it. I'll send an experienced assistant editor in to help you with the day-to-day details, but I want your ideas to give the magazine a fresh view."

Clara stood silently. Could she handle this job? She had been editor of her high school paper. *That's a little bit different,* her conscience reasoned. There was her work on the *Rag. With an experienced assistant editor I could handle it,* she silently argued back. Stacey interrupted her thoughts.

"The magazine headquarters will be in Los Angeles. Belinda would have a much wider base for public speaking."

"I don't know," Clara said hesitantly. She knew she wanted the job, but what would Belinda say about moving?

"Look, think about it. Talk it over with Belinda, and if you decide tonight, let me know. If not, then give me a call next week back at the office." She reached into her pocket and handed Clara a business card. Smiling confidently, she added, "Diana failed to mention how beautiful you are. I'm looking forward to working with you." She left before a stunned Clara could reply.

Clara gazed at the card for some time. She had a job. After all those years of wanting to work, she finally had a job. And in publishing no less! She had to find Belinda to tell her. She craned her neck and eventually spotted Belinda on the other side of the room. She pushed forward until Belinda looked up and Clara waved. They made their way across the crowded room to each other.

Belinda took Clara's hand and pulled her toward a corner. Excitedly, Belinda turned and said, "You're never going to believe what just happened." Without waiting, Belinda rushed on. "I've just been asked to go on a nationwide tour with the Women's/Lesbians' Rights Team. They're scheduled to go across the country speaking out for our rights." Belinda grasped her head. "Can you believe it? What's wrong?" she asked when Clara didn't respond.

The card Stacey had given her bit into her palm as she crumpled it.

"Don't look so sad," Belinda said. "You'll travel with me."

Travel with her, Clara thought. She wouldn't be able to take the job.

"Clara, if you'd rather I didn't . . ."

"No," she said quickly, forcing a smile. "I'm sorry. I guess it just caught me by surprise. What about your job at the insurance company?"

"I'll have to take a leave of absence or quit," Belinda said, still watching her. "Let's go outside," she suggested.

They walked quietly across the massive lawn for some time before stopping beneath a large, fragrant magnolia tree. The night was soft and warm; the faint sound of music and laughter floated from the house. Belinda leaned against the tree and pulled Clara to her, kissing her softly. "What's wrong?"

Clara still held the crumpled card in her hand.

105

Tears stung her eyes as she told her about Stacey Benson's offer.

"Darling, that's great," Belinda exclaimed, hugging her.

"I can't take the job," Clara said with a sniff.

"Why not?" When she didn't answer, Belinda continued, "You know how much I love you, and I know you love me. But if you give up this opportunity to follow me from city to city you'll soon hate me."

Clara started to protest, but Belinda covered her mouth with her hand. "No, baby, listen to me. You'd soon resent having to tag along, and if I give up this chance and follow you I'd grow to resent you for stopping me. Take the job. We can still see each other occasionally. It's not forever."

Clara's throat ached from the unshed tears. They held each other tightly.

"We've always known, haven't we?" Belinda whispered, hugging Clara closer. Clara could only nod as she buried her face against Belinda's neck. It had been a great year, but they both knew things would never be the same. Their time together was over.

CHAPTER EIGHT

A week later Clara left, waving good-bye to Belinda from the airport window in Shreveport. She was met at the Los Angeles airport by Stacey Benson and her new assistant editor, Elaine Adams. Elaine was a short woman with long curly hair the color of ripe wheat. After the introductions were made, Elaine drove them to the magazine office. Clara was tired but eager to begin her new job. Her head was already buzzing with new ideas.

"Elaine worked with me in New York," Stacey explained. "She'll take good care of you."

"You'll love it," Elaine chirped. "There's nothing like watching a magazine develop into a finished product."

Clara was suddenly consumed with fear and self-doubt. Why had she ever agreed to take the job? She wasn't qualified. "I hope we don't all live to regret this," she murmured from the backseat of the car.

Stacey was sitting sideways in the front seat and turned to look at her closely. "You'll be fine," she said with a smile.

They stopped in front of a small, two-story building. "This is it," Elaine announced. "Home of the new and improved *Woman's View*." She practically bounced out of the car.

Clara followed more slowly and stood looking up at the slightly dilapidated building. "How much authority do I have as editor?" she asked, turning to Stacey and wondering why they didn't hear her pounding heart.

"Well," Stacey said, hesitating a bit, "short of selling the business, I suppose we could say absolute — within reason, of course," she added with a slightly nervous-sounding laugh.

"My first decision as editor is to rename the magazine *Sappho's Digest*," Clara said. "*Woman's View* sounds like something my mother would read."

"Whoa!" Stacey held up her hands. "You have no idea how much paperwork that would cause."

"I want it changed," Clara insisted. "If it's going to be a new magazine, it deserves a new name. Keeping the old one doesn't suggest a new product."

Elaine stood quietly watching the two women.

When Stacey didn't answer, Clara turned back to the car. "Drive me back to the airport."

"Wait a minute!" Stacey yelled, running after her. "It's that important to you?" she asked, catching her arm.

"If the job hadn't been important to me I wouldn't have given up Belinda for it," she replied evenly.

"Look, I never meant to cause you any problems with this job. If I have, I'm truly sorry." She dropped her hand from Clara's arm.

"Once something runs its course, it's better to move on," Clara admitted, turning to open the car door.

"Don't you want to see the editor's office for *Sappho's Digest* before we leave?" Stacey asked with raised eyebrows and a slight smile.

Clara's breath caught for the briefest moment at Stacey's expression. For one tiny second it had looked so much like Randi. She pushed the thought away. "What about all that paperwork?"

"I pay a fortune for accounting and legal advice. They'll handle it."

Elaine breathed a heavy sigh of relief, causing Clara and Stacey to laugh. "Goddess, you two scared me. I thought I was going to have to go back to New York and beg for my apartment back."

They walked through the quiet building. "When do you want the first edition out?" Clara asked.

"Two months," Stacey replied.

"That's pretty short notice," Elaine yelped. "We don't even have a staff yet."

Stacey waved her hand to dismiss the problem. "You have an editor, an assistant editor, a brand-new name, and your staff will be here bright and early tomorrow morning. Now let me buy you both dinner. We can start work first thing tomorrow."

They enjoyed a leisurely meal before returning to their hotel. Elaine's room was on the floor below theirs. Clara and Stacey rode up in silence. "How about a drink?" Stacey offered, stepping off the elevator.

"It's getting late," Clara replied, well aware of the faint attraction she had for Stacey. "I'm sure you're exhausted."

"No, but you probably are. I should've thought about that." Stacey dug into her pocket for her door key.

"Actually, I'm so wired about this job I may never sleep." Clara laughed nervously. She was definitely having thoughts about Stacey that weren't professional.

"Then come in for a drink."

Clara again noticed her soft brown eyes. They seemed to hold a hidden promise that made her want to delve deeper and find what was there. "All right."

Stacey called room service and had a bottle of wine sent up. They chatted about ideas Clara had for the magazine until the wine arrived.

Stacey poured them a glass and sat next to Clara on the sofa. "I'm really sorry about the problems with Belinda."

"I think we both always knew we weren't meant

to be together forever. I'll always love her dearly. She's my best friend."

"So you're a free woman then?" Stacey looked at her over her wine glass.

Clara felt the heat building within her. It had been less than twenty-four hours since she had left Belinda's bed, and she was already lusting after someone else. Confused by her emotions, she busied herself studying her glass. "We've agreed that we're free to date other women if we want to." Clara could sense Stacey staring at her.

"Clara, I hate playing games," she said, gently brushing back the hair from Clara's forehead. "Would you spend the night with me?"

Startled, Clara turned to her to say no, but she was met by smoldering eyes that left no doubt about Stacey's desire. The very intensity of the look caused her breath to catch. Without planning to, Clara leaned toward her and kissed her softly. They pulled away and Stacey set their glasses down. Their lips blended together in an inferno of need. Clara's hands ran rampant over Stacey's short, blond hair. Stacey was almost young enough to be her daughter. Clara was about to voice that fact when Stacey's hand began to massage her breast. At that point, all doubt faded.

"It's more comfortable in here," Stacey murmured, leading Clara to the bedroom. "You're a beautiful woman," she whispered, removing Clara's jacket.

Stacey slowly undressed Clara and gazed down at her. "You really don't realize how beautiful you are, do you?" Stacey said and quickly shed her own clothes to lie down beside Clara.

"I'm afraid I dim in your presence," Clara replied, taking in the slender but well-muscled body beside her.

"I want to kiss every inch of you," Stacey whispered. "I want to hear you moan and scream in pleasure."

Clara soon discovered it wasn't at all difficult to fulfill Stacey's wishes. It seemed that Stacey was everywhere at once, stroking, kissing, probing, or sucking on Clara's body. They still hadn't slept when Elaine called Stacey for breakfast. Stacey made a muffled excuse and asked Elaine to meet her at the office later.

"Sleep," Stacey said, after hanging up the phone, "while I take a shower."

"I'm not tired," Clara said, stretching. "I'm starving to death. I'll go to my room and get ready and meet you back here in thirty minutes for breakfast."

"You're on." Stacey kissed her deeply.

"Don't do that," Clara warned, "or we'll have to start all over."

"In that case there's only one thing for me to do," Stacey said in a low husky voice.

"Yeah?" Clara said, smiling wickedly and arching her body to meet Stacey's. "And what might that be?"

Smiling, Stacey put her hands against Clara and with a shove rolled her off the bed. Stacey roared with laughter.

"There's no dignity sitting naked on the floor," Clara replied. "Help me up." Innocently she held out her hands. Stacey was soon in a heap beside her.

"You're absolutely right," Stacey agreed, laughing as Clara rolled on top of her. Once more their breaths caught as they stared into each other's eyes. "Clara," Stacey moaned, "if you don't stop moving against me like that you're going to be late for your first day at work."

"Do you think they'll report me to my boss?" Clara continued to grind herself against her.

"It's possible." She grinned. "I hear old Benson is a real hard-ass."

"Oh, I don't know. I kind of like her ass myself." Clara leered, pushing her thigh between Stacey's legs.

It was after nine before Stacey and Clara arrived for work. Elaine and the new staff for *Sappho's Digest* were drinking coffee at a large table littered with empty doughnut boxes. Two extra chairs were found and brought in. Clara took the one next to Elaine, who gave her a crooked smile. "I tried to call you for breakfast," she whispered.

Clara felt her face redden. "I must have been in the shower," she stammered.

"That was exactly what I told myself," Elaine said, grinning wickedly.

Clara chuckled, knowing she and Elaine were going to be good friends.

Stacey got the group's attention, and as each

person introduced herself and gave a brief rundown of her job skills, Clara jotted notes and silently made decisions on ways to best utilize each woman's talents.

After the introductions, Stacey gave a brief account of the paper's history before turning the meeting over to Clara.

Nervously, Clara pulled her notes out and outlined some of her ideas for revamping the magazine. Her insecurities were forgotten as the other women began to toss out ideas. When they grew hungry, Stacey had pizzas delivered. By late afternoon, the exhausted group had hammered out a preliminary format.

Clara thanked the staff members as they left, letting each of them know how happy she was to be working with her.

Alone, Clara, Stacey, and Elaine collapsed at the table. "I'm exhausted," Elaine moaned, rubbing her neck.

"Me, too," Clara yawned. Last night's lack of sleep was catching up with her. She turned to see Stacey's soft brown eyes questioning her, and her exhaustion vanished in a sharp wave of desire. She smiled in return.

"How about some dinner," Stacey asked, turning to Elaine.

Elaine began gathering her papers. "I can't. I'm meeting an old college friend. She's going to take me dancing and introduce me to the wonderful women of Los Angeles." She sighed enthusiastically.

"All of them?" Clara teased.

"Far be it from me to deprive even a single woman the opportunity to sample the nectar from my lush garden," she intoned, drawing a wrist to her forehead and striking a dramatic pose.

"Well, just make sure you aren't caught sampling someone else's chosen fruit," Stacey warned, laughing.

Elaine gave Stacey a knowing look and retorted, "Make sure you're on time tomorrow." Walking out the door, she flung over her shoulder, "And try to let her get some sleep tonight. I don't want to watch her yawning all day tomorrow."

"Was she talking to you or me?" Clara asked after the door closed.

"Both of us, I think."

"I am tired," Clara admitted, stretching the kinks out of her back.

"I give a great back rub," Stacey said, strolling behind Clara and massaging her shoulders. "We could order from room service and discuss today's meeting." Her lips lightly traced Clara's ear.

"Sounds like an excellent idea," Clara moaned as Stacey's lips trailed down her neck.

Stacey stayed in Los Angeles for another week, helped Clara find an apartment, and assisted in getting her settled. They spent their nights together. Clara knew she would miss her, but there was still a small feeling of relief when Stacey returned to New York. At last, Clara was alone to start her new life.

The morning Stacey left, Clara called a staff meeting. She watched the eleven women walk in and find seats. Most had worked on the old magazine; only two were as inexperienced as she was. She waited until they settled down. Taking a deep breath, she stood and began.

"We have fifty-five days to plan, lay out, and distribute our first issue. I've studied each of your skills and experience and have decided to place you where I think you'll be most valuable for now. Joan," she called to a petite woman sitting in the corner, "I want you to pull the files of our predecessor and send a letter to each of its subscribers telling them that we intend to honor their old subscriptions." She saw Elaine's frown but continued. "Ruth," she nodded to a big, muscular woman, "I want you to design a flyer describing the magazine and post it in every lesbian bar and bookstore you can find within a day's drive from here and mail copies of it to every lesbian business you can get an address for in the country." There was a series of hoots and numerous offers to help Ruth search out the bars and bookstores. Clara smiled and looked next at the short, quiet woman with eyes that could melt the soul of Anita Bryant herself. "Alice," she continued, "I want you to start calling and writing every lesbian establishment and organization you can find and get them to run an ad in our classified section. Offer them a ten percent discount if they'll run for six months and fifteen percent for a one-year run. Marie," she said to the tall, gangly woman with short frizzy hair, "I have a list of writers here. I want you to call — not write — call everyone on the list and solicit works from them." Clara continued around the room until each woman was assigned a task. Finally, she dismissed them, and they all filed out talking excitedly among themselves. Elaine sat at the table playing with her pen.

"Something wrong?" Clara asked, seeing her frowning.

"You just spent a hell of a lot of money."

"I expect to make a lot, too." Clara defended.

"And if you don't?"

Clara picked up her notebook before replying. "Then you'll have to break in a new editor and I'll be selling pencils on the corner."

As the days passed, the building became a constant hum of activity. Phone calls and mail started coming in; subscriptions and advertisements were building daily. Articles, poems, artwork, short stories, and photographs poured in. Stacey had said she would be satisfied with eighty pages per issue for the first year of printing. The first issue of *Sappho's Digest* was one hundred and twenty-eight pages with a circulation of nine thousand. They had to recruit volunteers to help with the mailing, and two days before deadline, the magazine was mailed. Clara threw a small party for the staff and volunteers. It was going in full swing when she went to her tiny office and called Stacey.

"We just mailed the first issue," she said proudly when Stacey answered the phone.

"I knew you could do it." She laughed joyously. "Damn, I wish you were here. I'd show you my gratitude all night long."

"Well, don't thank me yet. Wait until you get the profit reports. I've discovered I like spending other people's money."

"Do I have enough to buy a plane ticket from New York to Los Angeles?"

"Probably, but don't," Clara said quietly.

"Why not? I miss you."

"That's exactly why. I miss you too. One absentee lover is all I can handle right now."

"How is Belinda?" Stacey's voice was dry.

"Fine. She called me from Florida last night. They were going to South Carolina from there."

"Did you tell her about us?"

"Yes. I told you we agreed that we should be seeing other people." She didn't add that Belinda had been mentioning a woman named Sandy in her letters more and more frequently.

"When will they reach California?" Stacey asked.

"In about nine months. They end their tour in San Francisco."

"I wish I'd made Elaine editor," Stacey said suddenly.

"Why?" Clara's self-doubt nagged at her as she toyed with her pen. "Am I not doing the job you expected?"

"You're doing a great job. I just want you here with me."

"Don't, Stacey. We both knew how it would be before we got involved."

"Yeah, I just didn't know how involved I was getting."

"I have to go. I'm running up my boss's phone bill."

"You may as well run up her phone bill. You've

already run up her temperature about thirty degrees."
Stacey moaned.

Clara laughed deep within her throat. "Well, if
you're willing to lend me a hand, there's something I
can do about that. Just listen to what I would do to
you right now if you were here."

Forty minutes later Clara rejoined the party
flushed and smiling.

CHAPTER NINE

The next day Clara sat staring out the window of
her apartment. A soft breeze blew the curtain gently.
In her lap she had a letter from Belinda. It was the
one she had been expecting and dreading for so long.
Shortly after they hit the road, Belinda began to
mention Sandy in her letters. Each one contained
more and more references to her. Today's letter told
her that they were lovers and that Belinda wouldn't
be moving to California. Clara was upset that Belinda

would be so far away from her, but she felt nothing but a deep love and gratitude for her friendship. She wondered briefly if there was something wrong with her, if some element was missing that prevented her from being able to maintain a relationship. She gently probed her feelings for Stacey. She cared deeply for Stacey, but did she love her? The phone jarred her from her thoughts.

"Hello."

"Hi, it's me."

"Belinda!"

"Yeah, I thought I'd better give you a ring." She hesitated. "Did you get my letter?"

"Yes. Today."

"I know I shouldn't have written to tell you, but you know what a coward I am. Are you angry with me?" Belinda's voice sound strained.

"No. We were right for each other for a while, but not forever. You'll still be my friend, won't you?" Clara asked. Tears burned her eyes, but she refused to let herself cry.

"Try and stop me." She heard Belinda sniff. "I'll miss talking to you."

"You have my number, and you'd better keep calling. I'd like to meet Sandy when you come to San Francisco. Please come to see me."

"You've got yourself a date. Clara . . ." She hesitated.

"Yes?"

"Call Randi."

"I can't." The tears rolled freely down her cheeks.

"You never got over her. I always knew that.

Don't spend your life running from woman to woman when you've already found the one who's right for you."

I don't exactly run from woman to woman, she wanted to reply. But instead she said, "Bye, Belinda."

"Bye, baby. Write me."

Clara sat staring out the window for several minutes. She was confused by her mixed feelings for Belinda. She knew she had never loved her the way she loved Randi, but Belinda would always be special. She hoped Sandy could give her the happiness she deserved.

Was Belinda right? Should she call Randi? For a brief, electrifying moment, she remembered how Randi's hands felt caressing her back. How her hot breath had burned against her . . . Clara jumped up and began to work on a new proposal for a series she was thinking about. Work was what she needed.

Clara slammed the phone down in disgust.

"What's wrong now?" Elaine asked. Clara could hear the exhaustion in her voice.

"That was Marie. She's sick and needs somebody to replace her tonight."

"What's she got going?"

"I don't know." Grabbing a work schedule, Clara ran over the list. "She has an interview at nine tonight with some painter."

"Which one?"

"You know how Marie fills out her work schedule. It just says *Interview painter — 9 p.m. — Blue Moon*

Gallery. For all I know, it may be a house painter."
Clara groaned.

The sixth issue of *Sappho's Digest* was due to lay-out the next day, and every disaster possible had occurred. Over half of the staff was out with some kind of virus that had slowly been making its rounds in the office.

"Why don't you send Liz?" Elaine offered.

"She's helping Angie rewrite that story on the Gay Rights Bill that Congress just shot the hell out of." Clara lit a cigarette and rubbed her temple.

"What about Lucy?"

"She had to leave. Her daughter's sick."

"How about —"

"Forget it," Clara interrupted. "I've already checked everyone. They're either home sick or already doing their own jobs and two others. I'll go myself."

"What do you know about art?" Elaine queried.

Clara leaned back in her chair and placed her feet on the corner of her desk. She closed her eyes and smoked her cigarette slowly. "I can tell a killdeer from a plover," she answered softly.

She seldom allowed herself to think of Randi anymore. Any time Randi's memory pushed in, Clara would find more work to do to blot it out. She had tried dating a couple of women, but it hadn't worked out. She still maintained a phone relationship with Stacey, but their busy schedules and the vast geographical distance between them hadn't allowed them to see each other since Clara had arrived in Los Angeles. She again wondered about her seeming preference for superficial relationships. "Elaine, can I ask you a personal question?"

"Sure. It doesn't mean I'll answer it, but you can ask."

"How many women have you slept with?"

Elaine walked over next to the desk. "Is that a proposition?"

Opening her eyes, Clara found the wide, candid smile she had grown to love. "No," she answered, grinning back.

"In that case, not nearly enough."

"You're not going to tell me, are you?"

"Nope."

"Thanks."

"For what?"

"Not depressing me anymore than I already am," Clara said, swinging her feet off the desk and standing up. "I'm going home and sleep for a while, and then I'm going to go interview that painter."

"Sure you won't change your mind on that proposition?" Elaine teased.

"No. You youngsters wear me out."

"See you tomorrow, Granny."

Laughing, Clara shot her the bird and left the office. Back in her apartment, she fixed herself a cup of hot tea and crawled into a hot bath. Why was she so miserable? She should be happy. The magazine, despite the last three days, was doing great. Subscriptions continued to climb, and she and Elaine had developed some great new additions for future issues. So why so glum? she asked herself, sliding lower into the tub. Maybe she *should* have propositioned Elaine.

"No." She scoffed out loud. They worked so close together they would spend the entire night discussing the magazine. Maybe someone else then? She remembered the photographer she had met last week at a party. She had certainly been sending Clara all of the right signals. Now *she* was a possibility. Clara yawned loudly. But right now what she really needed was sleep. Finishing her tea, she stood and dried herself. She was soon asleep, stretched out across her bed.

The alarm clock jangled madly in her ear. Irritated, Clara slapped it off and pulled herself up. She forced herself to stand in a cold shower to wake up. Dressing quickly, she left for the interview. The exhibit was being held at a privately-owned gallery. Clara was surprised by the large number of people in attendance — mostly women. Glancing around at some of the paintings, she realized why so many people were present. The works were beautiful. She stopped to study one of a woman reclining on a large rock, staring out across the sea. There was something vaguely disturbing about the woman. She was trying to decipher it when the murmuring from a cluster of people nearby caught her attention.

She made her way over to the crowd and found herself staring at a painting of two women embracing. One woman was facing her. There was a look of such complete sexual arousal, that Clara felt herself growing wet. She felt pulled to the painting; there was something so familiar. A tingling sensation ran up her spine and teased the hairs on the back of her neck as she realized who the artist was. Turning, she fled from the room, tears blinding her. The damp night air hit her as she rushed from the building and began to run to her car. She had only gone a few feet when she ran into someone. Arms closed around her and kept her from falling.

"I'm sorry," she mumbled. Clara looked up to find herself staring into soft gray eyes. Her knees weakened, and the arms tightened around her, holding her. An eternity passed between them. She tried to find her voice, but her throat seemed to have closed. Randi was molded to her. Clara could feel Randi's heat scorching the length of her body. *This is where I belong,* her mind screamed. Her lips ached to kiss Randi. Her hands slowly lowered on their own volition until they closed around Randi's hips and pulled her closer. She almost shouted with joy when she heard Randi's breath catch and saw her eyes darken with desire. Randi leaned into her, her eyes locked on Clara's lips.

"There you are," a deep, drawling voice called. Randi pulled away abruptly. Clara almost fell from the sudden release. "I've been looking all over for you. Everyone's asking for you." Clara watched the tall, gorgeous blond wrap her arms around Randi. She looked down at Clara. "Oh, I didn't realize you were busy," she said with a pout.

"Joyce," Randi murmured, "this is Clara Webster. Clara, Joyce Roberts."

"Are you going to the exhibit?" Joyce asked, eyeing Clara suspiciously.

Clara cleared her throat and was amazed at how calm her voice sounded. How could she sound this calm when everything inside her was dissolving into nothing? "No, actually I'm the editor of *Sappho's*

Digest. I thought I might be able to interview Ms. Kosub."

"Sorry, babe, but Randi's going to be tied up all night," she said, pulling Randi possessively closer. Clara felt as though she had been kicked in the stomach.

"Some other time perhaps," Clara choked, quickly walking away. She felt ill. She had to get away from them. She rushed to her car and drove back to the office. The building was empty, and shadows danced forlornly on the walls. Going to her office, she flipped the lights on, fell into her chair, and pushed away the tears that threatened to start again.

Her body still burned from the feel of Randi's touch. Angry with herself, Clara pushed the thoughts away and focused on the magazine. The magazine was her life now. Randi was history. Randi was with someone else. She shoved the thought away. She had failed to get an interview with Randi and something would have to fill that blank. She remembered the haunting portrait. Picking up her pen, Clara pulled a pad of paper toward her. Quickly she wrote down her reaction to Randi's painting and briefly touched on Randi's gentle personality. She closed with her wish that the world would soon recognize Randi Kosub for the brilliant artist she is. Sitting down at a computer, Clara carefully typed out the story. Laying the finished copy aside, she lit a cigarette and breathed a sigh of relief. The sixth issue of *Sappho's Digest* was ready for layout. Only then did she allow herself to sit back and think of Randi, and she didn't try to stop the tears.

* * * * *

"Clara! Clara wake up."

Raising her head from her arms, Clara gazed at the blurry outline of Elaine.

"What are you doing here at this time of morning?" Elaine demanded.

"I wanted to finish that article. What time is it?"

"A little after six. Have you been here all night?"

Clara looked at her watch, confused. "I guess I fell asleep."

"Is everything all right? You look terrible."

"Yeah, things are just great." She rubbed her face. Her eyes felt swollen, and she had a terrible headache. She started digging through her desk for a bottle of aspirin.

"What's wrong?"

"Headache," she whispered. She was crying again.

"Come on," Elaine said, taking her arm. "Let's get you out of here before someone else comes in."

Clara allowed herself to be led to Elaine's car. A short time later, soft and nurturing Elaine was tucking her into bed. Clara heard her digging through the medicine cabinet. "Where do you keep your aspirin?" she asked, coming back into the bedroom.

"On the windowsill in the kitchen."

Elaine returned with two aspirin and a glass of water. "Rest now. I've unplugged the phone so no one will bother you." Clara didn't hear her leave.

Clara woke to the smell of coffee perking and bacon frying. The clock beside her bed showed it was already after two. Slowly she got out of bed and slipped on her robe. Walking into the kitchen, she found Elaine filling a coffee cup. "You didn't have to stay."

"I didn't. I went back to the office long enough to make sure everything there was under control. As of noon we were back on schedule, and nearly everyone has returned to work. Then I came over to check on you. Sit down." She filled another cup and handed it to Clara. She turned back to the stove.

"What do you have there?" Clara asked.

"Biscuits."

"Biscuits!"

"Yeah, I'm starving and felt like eating breakfast. Since you wouldn't get up and cook for me, I had to make do for myself. I'm a woman of great resources, you know."

Clara got up and helped set the table. They laughed and chatted about the magazine while they ate. "That was a great article you wrote on Randi Kosub," Elaine said, stacking the dishes in the sink.

"Thanks."

Elaine was eyeing her. "What's she like?" She washed dishes while Clara dried them and slowly launched into details of Randi's personality. When she fell silent for several minutes Elaine asked, "Do you want to talk about what's wrong?"

Clara looked down at her and shook her head. "Elaine, you've been wonderful, but I'm not ready yet."

"I understand." She was drying her hands on a dish towel when someone knocked on the door.

"Who can that be?" Clara said with a frown.

"Probably a salesman." Elaine grimaced.

Clara looked down at her robe. "Can you answer it and get rid of whoever it is?"

"Sure. You just sit back and watch how I handle these characters." With an exaggerated swagger, she twirled the dish towel and walked to the door.

Clara could hear voices but couldn't distinguish what was being said. She heard Elaine call her.

"Who is it?" she asked, stepping out of the kitchen.

Elaine stood back and opened the door wider. Clara felt her knees go weak at the sight of Randi.

Randi looked from Elaine to Clara. Clara saw her eyes take in the robe and suddenly she was gone.

Clara ran to the door and yelled for her to wait, but she was already down the stairs. Clara ran after her but couldn't catch her. She walked slowly back up to her second floor apartment where Elaine was still standing at the door. She closed it softly as Clara collapsed on the couch.

"Damn!" Clara slammed her fists against her knees. "Why wouldn't she stop?"

"Maybe she didn't expect to find me here and you in your robe at this time of day."

Clara covered her face with her hands and sighed. She was too tired. With a little pressure, she told Elaine about Randi and Allen. When she had finished, the room was bathed in the first shadows of evening. Wearily she stood and turned a lamp on. "I've wasted your entire day," she apologized.

"Nonsense, that's what friends are for." She bounced up. "Let's go out somewhere. What would you like to do?"

"I'm too tired."

"No you're not. You're depressed. Get up, take a

shower, and get dressed. Come on," she prodded. "What sounds like fun?"

Elaine's insistence caused Clara to laugh. "You're a bigger nuisance than a puppy."

She tossed her head. "But I'm twice as cute, and I rarely pee on the floor."

"All right. Give me a few minutes." Clara emerged a short time later wearing a white cotton shirt and jeans.

Elaine whistled. "On second thought, why don't we just stay in?"

Clara shook her head, suddenly anxious to be out of the tiny apartment. "Let's go by that new bar we've been hearing raves about. I want to dance and get really drunk. Then I want you to bring me home, put me to bed and, like a good friend, sleep on the couch."

"You really had my interest until that sleeping on the couch bit. Always the friend, never the lover," she said, holding her hand to her forehead dramatically.

"Who needs lovers when they have a friend like you?" Clara kissed her lightly on the cheek.

Elaine frowned. "I'm not sure that was a compliment, but let's go."

It was early morning before a nearly-equally drunk Elaine dumped Clara unceremoniously on her bed. Clara lay clutching the sheet, willing the room to stop spinning.

"Goddess, you're heavy," Elaine cried.

"It's rude to tell a lady she's fat," Clara mumbled.

"I didn't say fat. I said heavy." Silence hung between them. Clara opened her eyes to find Elaine leaning over staring at her. Elaine's lips brushed against hers gently.

"It would never work," Clara said tenderly.

"But think of the fun we could have tonight."

"We're both too drunk. Come on. Lie down and hold me." Clara scooted over, and Elaine stretched out beside her on her back. Elaine's shorter body alongside her felt different but interesting to Clara.

"Not even a couple of quick feels?" Elaine asked, laughing.

"I'd be asleep before you could get turned over." Clara lay quietly for a moment. She didn't want Elaine to think she was actually rejecting her. "Elaine, you've been teasing, haven't you? I mean you're not really considering us together?"

Clara waited for an answer, but all she heard was Elaine's even breathing. "Great," she growled, "you go to sleep just when I'm ready to consider your offer." Turning onto her side she cuddled against the sleeping form and fell asleep.

"How are you feeling?" Elaine chirped, walking into Clara's office late the next morning. She had been gone when Clara woke.

"Horny, thanks to a certain tease I know," she grumbled.

"Tease indeed. I practically got on my knees," Elaine protested.

"Then fell asleep just as I was ready to succumb to your charm."

"Hey, I'm a woman of action. I can't spend the entire night waiting for you to give in," she said with

132

a wink. "We're sending out for doughnuts. Do you want one?"

"Yeah."

Elaine turned to leave. "Clara, are you all right? You still look pretty bad."

"Great. I'm fat when you're drunk and ugly when you're sober." Seeing the concern on Elaine's face, she smiled and added. "I'm fine. Just keep me busy."

"That I can handle," came a voice from the doorway.

They looked up to find Stacey standing there.

"What are you doing here?" Elaine asked. Clara could hear the surprise in her voice.

"I came to see how my favorite editor and her ever-so-charming assistant editor are doing. How about some breakfast?"

"I can't," Elaine answered, almost too quickly, Clara thought. "I have to check on a dozen things this morning. I'll see you two later." She slipped out the door, closing it behind her.

"She'll never get an award for being subtle." Stacey chuckled, coming around the desk to Clara and sitting on her lap. "I've missed you," she whispered as she kissed her gently.

"I've missed you, too," Clara said, wishing Stacey had not chosen this time to fly out.

"You're looking tired. Have you been sick?"

"No. Elaine and I did a little too much celebrating last night."

"Oh?" she asked, arching her eyebrow. "Do I have competition?"

"No, not really. There's just Elaine, Sara, Jo Ann, Mary, Jen . . ."

Stacey kissed her silent. "Let's get out of here."

"I thought you came to visit the magazine."

"You can tell me all about it later. If you don't get me out of here soon, I'm going to have you right here in this chair."

"Might be an interesting thought," Clara replied and smiled wickedly. "Let's go."

Later in Clara's apartment, they lay wrapped in each other's arms. Stacey kissed the top of Clara's head.

"Do you want to talk about it?" Stacey asked.

"About what?"

"*Whatever* or *whoever* has you a million miles away."

Clara raised up on her elbow. "I'm sorry." She ran her hand over Stacey's spiked hair. "I love your hair. Did I ever tell you that?" Her chest constricted and tears filled her eyes.

"Talk to me," Stacey prompted.

Clara sat up and pulled the sheet around her. She told Stacey about Randi, Allen, and Belinda. She told Stacey of her fears of being a failure, of not being able to maintain a relationship. She told her how she had failed as a mother and even told her of the fears she had of failing as an editor. When she was silent, Stacey pulled her back down into her arms. "Clara, Allen's an arrogant bastard. Your concern for the boys and Randi's career cost you Randi. Your career and Belinda's clashed. None of these things are a bad reflection on you. As for being a bad mother, I think you're feeling sorry for yourself." Clara started to rise to protest, but Stacey pulled her back down. "Listen to me," she said sternly. "The boys grew up. They no longer required your hovering and constant attention."

Clara looked away. Deep down she knew Stacey was right about her need for the boys to remain dependent on her, but it still hadn't made it any easier for her.

Stacey rubbed her back and continued. "I'd be willing to bet that if you keep calling and writing they'll eventually come around. And for your skills as an editor," Stacey said, pulling away and sitting up, "you're already a much better editor than I'll ever be."

"Bullshit!"

"I mean it. You took a pile of paper and turned it into a magazine that begs to be read. People love it. I'm going to miss you," she stated, looking into Clara's eyes.

"What do you mean?"

Stacey crawled out of bed and began getting dressed.

"Stacey, are you angry?"

"Angry?" Stacey asked frowning. "Yes and no. I'm angry with myself for not being able to elicit the kind of love from you that you have for Randi. But I'm not angry with you. I'm sad to see you leave."

"But I'm not leaving."

"Yes you are. You're going to go find Randi and the happiness you deserve. If she went to the trouble to find you here, she must still care. If you both want it bad enough, you'll work it out."

"I can't leave. I have a job here."

"What's more important, Randi or the magazine?

It's up and running now. The only challenge left is meeting monthly deadlines."

Clara slowly smoothed the sheet around her. Did she want to try with Randi? Would Randi be willing to try again?

"You still love her, don't you?" Stacey's voice carried a hollow sound.

Unable to speak, Clara nodded her head.

"Then find her and tell her."

"What if she doesn't want to see me?"

"Why don't you worry about that when and if it happens? Personally, I don't think it'll happen." She sighed and buttoned her shirt. "Let's get busy. We can have you out of here in a week — maybe less if we work hard."

"What about the magazine?"

Stacey stared at the ceiling thoughtfully. "You're promoted to director of our southern region."

"What the hell is that?" Clara asked, brushing away her tears.

"I expect to get a big thick packet of information from you each month on lesbian events and activities from your area. I'll want occasional articles from you for both of my magazines; plus, I expect you to be a glowing role model of lesbian love."

Crawling out of bed, Clara wrapped her arms around Stacey. "I love you," she whispered.

"If it doesn't work out, give me a call."

Clara was shocked to see tears in Stacey's eyes. "You're on, hot shot."

CHAPTER TEN

The next morning Clara made reservations for a flight to Shreveport for the following Thursday. Then she slowly worked up the courage to call Jamie and Roger. Jamie answered the phone.

"Jamie, it's me . . . your mom." Clara's hand shook so badly she was afraid she would drop the phone. Silence met her, and she rushed to fill it. "I want to come to see you. Will you see me?"

An eternity seemed to pass before he answered. "Dad won't like it, but yeah, I guess it's okay with me."

Clara felt her excitement begin to grow. "Will you bring Roger?"

"I'll tell him and let him decide."

"Fair enough," she answered, somewhat disappointed. "I'll be at the Holiday Inn on Covington on Thursday." They quickly agreed on a time and hung up.

Four days later, after a final farewell to Elaine and her staff, Clara left for Shreveport. Stacey had made Elaine editor of *Sappho's Digest*.

When the knock sounded on her hotel room door, Clara was close to panic. Instinct told her this could be her last chance to patch things up with her sons. Nervously she opened the door to Jamie. He looked so much like Allen that she almost slammed it shut. When she realized he was alone, she looked frantically down the hallway.

"He wouldn't come," Jamie said slowly.

Clara nodded and stepped back to let him in.

There was an awkward moment as they stood staring at each other. "Sit down." Clara motioned to one of the two chairs. "Thank you for coming," she said. There was a painful silence. "Are you in college?" He should have started a few weeks back. She had missed his high school graduation.

"No, I'm working for UPS. I want to be an architect, but Dad wants me to work for him so he's refusing to pay my tuition. My grades weren't good enough for a scholarship, so I'm going to start at a junior college and work my way through."

"I could help you," she offered.

"Thanks, but I've kind of gotten attached to the idea of doing it myself." He gave her a slow grin that brought back so many memories. She looked away quickly.

"You look different," he observed.

Clara reached up to her short hair that was now heavily streaked with gray. "I stopped coloring it."

"It's not just your hair. It's something else," he said with a shrug. "You look happy." They fell silent again.

"Why did you have to leave?" he blurted out.

Clara sighed and leaned back into her chair. "Jamie, your father was a very difficult man to live with."

"Is that why you became a lesbian?"

Clara was shocked by his question. She had trouble thinking of him as an adult. He was still her little boy.

He shifted uneasily in his chair. "I'm sorry. I shouldn't have said that." Clara felt a heavy burden slide from her shoulders as she stared at the young man in front of her. Jamie might look like his father, but that was where the resemblance stopped. She had had some influence on him after all.

"I don't mind talking about it, if you don't," she said, placing her hand over his.

For the next thirty minutes she answered his

questions about her decision to leave and her new life as honestly as she could. "Is there anything else?" she asked when he finally leaned back in his chair.

"No, I think I understand. Maybe I always did. Roger and I knew Dad treated you bad. I used to get angry with you because you didn't talk back to him."

"I wasn't raised to talk back. I didn't know how. Leaving Allen was hard. I had no job skills, no place to go, and it meant leaving you and Roger." The mention of Roger's name finally gave her the courage to ask. "Why didn't Roger come with you?"

Jamie cracked his knuckles and gave a short sigh. "He's just being weird." He paused. "Do you remember that last day you went to see him in the hospital?"

Clara nodded. The moment was branded in her memory for the rest of her life.

"Apparently Dad said something about Roger being a fag, and it scared the shit out of him. He's afraid if he sees you he'll suddenly start chasing men."

Clara felt the old anger began to grow inside her. "That's the most ridiculous thing I've ever heard," she retorted. "Just because I'm gay doesn't mean either of you boys will be." She wondered what she could do to help Roger.

"Yeah, well give him time. I think he'll eventually come around. He's just at that weird stage. I'll keep working on him." He shifted in his seat. "Dad remarried, you know."

Clara's eyebrows raised in surprise. "No, I didn't. Who did he marry?"

"Stephanie Henson. They worked together." Jamie

added, "I don't think it turned out quite like he expected." He suddenly grinned as if recalling a private joke. "After they were married she made him hire a housekeeper, then she redecorated the whole house and ran up some serious bills. Dad's still paying them off. She divorced him less than a year later."

"Well, good for her," Clara said, slapping the table beside her.

"He was passed over for promotion," he told her.

Clara knew how much that had hurt Allen. He had spent his entire career working toward becoming president of the company. "What happened?"

"He wouldn't say, but Stephanie said it was because old man Johnson was real pissed that Dad divorced you."

Gene Johnson was the owner of the company. She had met him on dozens of occasions, but he had never paid her any more attention than he did anyone else. "Why?"

"I don't know. I guess it's that image thing. Maybe he's opposed to divorce."

She shook her head. All the time her life had been coming together, Allen's had been falling apart. She felt a slight tinge of satisfaction.

"I've got to go," he said, standing.

Clara looked up at him. "I'm moving near Corpus Christi. Will you come and visit me?"

He smiled that slow easy grin again. "Lots of pretty girls down that way, I hear."

She smiled and stood. "You heard right," she said.

He opened up his arms and pulled her into them. Her head rested against his chest. She squeezed her eyes shut to block the tears. "I'll even drag little bro down with me," he promised gruffly. Clara realized he was struggling with his own emotions.

Clara flew into Corpus late the next afternoon. Even though Thanksgiving was just a few days away it was still hot. Clara changed into shorts before leaving the airport. She rented a car and started driving. The closer she got, the more nervous she became. What if Randi no longer lived at the beach house? She had said it was only temporary. What if she had another exhibit somewhere? What if her relationship with the blond was serious? If it was serious, she wouldn't have come looking for me, she reasoned. *Maybe she just wanted to talk,* a nagging voice persisted.

Clara shivered, recalling the look of desire in Randi's eyes that night in front of the gallery. "She still cares," she said adamantly. Clara was determined to win her back no matter what. Lisa and Rosie would know where Randi was. She would go to them and do whatever it took to find her.

When she reached the road that turned off to Randi's house, Clara was amazed to find several small wooden stands sitting alongside the road. Driving slowly she saw the stands were selling all kinds of tourist items. Her heart started pounding when she spied Randi's Jeep. She pulled in behind it and shut off the motor.

Clara got out of the car and was met by the sharp smell of the Gulf water. For a moment she closed her eyes and let herself become lost in the rhythmic flow of the tide. The sound of voices caught her attention, and she opened her eyes to scan the crowd. Her chest constricted at the sight of Randi standing several yards away with her back to her. Taking a deep breath, Clara started toward her. As she drew nearer she noticed Randi was talking to a man about two small paintings he was holding.

"How much do you want for these two?" she heard the man ask. A large sign over his head read twenty dollars each.

"They're thirty dollars each or two for fifty," Clara answered. She could hear her voice quavering.

Randi and the man turned together to stare at her. "I'm her partner," Clara said without taking her eyes off Randi.

"Well," he pondered. "That's fair I suppose. My wife will love them. I'll take both."

Clara watched amused as Randi fumbled with paper while trying to wrap the paintings. The man paid for his purchase and went on his way.

"You just cheated him out of ten dollars," Randi said.

"He should learn to pay attention. Besides, I have to do something to earn my keep."

Randi stared at her closely. "What about your job with the magazine?"

"I resigned," she replied.

Randi folded her arms across her chest, her eyes growing darker with anger. "Where's your friend?"

"If you had waited around a couple of minutes longer, I would've introduced you to her. She was my assistant editor. She came over to put me back together. It seems I have a tendency to become rattled over bumping into you."

"What about Allen?"

"We were divorced shortly after I went back. I never spent a single night with him after you left."

"Leaving wasn't my idea," Randi said sharply.

Clara took a deep breath and watched the tide roll out. "That was the stupidest mistake I've ever made. If it were possible, I would undo it. But, Randi, I can't reverse time."

Randi's anger was disappearing, and she began to nervously rearrange the display of paintings.

"Are you involved with the blond I saw you with at the opening?"

Randi's face reddened and she looked away. "Joyce? No. Not really. She lives in Los Angeles. She was just . . ." She let the sentence die.

"She seemed rather fond of you," Clara persisted.

"Why are you here?" Randi asked, ignoring the comment.

"Because I love you and want us to work things out. I'm not the same person you knew before." Clara could see the multitude of emotions washing across Randi's face.

Randi looked away, but not before Clara saw the indecision in her eyes. "I can't play games," Randi said. "I want a forever relationship." She ran a hand through her hair.

"I want the same thing. With you," Clara stated.

They stood staring at each other. Clara hid her trembling hands by shoving them into the pockets of her shorts, while Randi stared at the crashing waves.

Clara tried to swallow, but her throat was too dry. "Randi, I've tried wrapping my life up in work and getting involved with someone else. Both were fine for a short time, but neither gave me what you did. I love you. Please don't turn me away unless you truly want me out of your life."

Randi stared at her for several seconds, and Clara's heart pounded fearfully through each of them.

"I'll need time." Randi's voice shook.

"I understand. Take all you need, because I'm not going anywhere."

After what seemed like an eternity, Randi took a tentative step forward and Clara went to meet her. They held each other tightly, oblivious to the stares from the people passing by.

A few of the publications of
THE NAIAD PRESS, INC.
P.O. Box 10543   Tallahassee, Florida 32302
Phone (850) 539-5965
Toll-Free Order Number: 1-800-533-1973
Mail orders welcome. Please include 15% postage.
Write or call for our free catalog which also features an
incredible selection of lesbian videos.

RHYTHM TIDE by Frankie J. Jones. 160 pp. . . . to desire
passionately and be passionately desired.   ISBN 1-56280-189-9 $11.95

PENN VALLEY PHOENIX by Janet McClellan. 208 pp. 2nd
Tru North Mystery.   ISBN 1-56280-200-3   11.95

BY RESERVATION ONLY by Jackie Calhoun. 240 pp. A
chance for true happiness.   ISBN 1-56280-191-0   11.95

OLD BLACK MAGIC by Jaye Maiman. 272 pp. 9th Robin
Miller Mystery.   ISBN 1-56280-175-9   11.95

LEGACY OF LOVE by Marianne K. Martin. 240 pp. Women
will do anything for her . . .   ISBN 1-56280-184-8   11.95

LETTING GO by Ann O'Leary. 160 pp. Laura, at 39, in love
with 23-year-old Kate.   ISBN 1-56280-183-X   11.95

LADY BE GOOD edited by Barbara Grier and Christine Cassidy.
288 pp. Erotic stories by Naiad Press authors.   ISBN 1-56280-180-5   14.95

CHAIN LETTER by Claire McNab. 288 pp. 9th Carol Ashton
mystery.   ISBN 1-56280-181-3   11.95

NIGHT VISION by Laura Adams. 256 pp. Erotic fantasy romance
by "famous" author.   ISBN 1-56280-182-1   11.95

SEA TO SHINING SEA by Lisa Shapiro. 256 pp. Unable to resist
the raging passion . . .   ISBN 1-56280-177-5   11.95

THIRD DEGREE by Kate Calloway. 224 pp. 3rd Cassidy James
mystery.   ISBN 1-56280-185-6   11.95

WHEN THE DANCING STOPS by Therese Szymanski. 272 pp.
1st Brett Higgins mystery.   ISBN 1-56280-186-4   11.95

PHASES OF THE MOON by Julia Watts. 192 pp. . . . . . hungry
for everything life has to offer.   ISBN 1-56280-176-7   11.95

BABY IT'S COLD by Jaye Maiman. 256 pp. 5th Robin Miller
mystery.   ISBN 1-56280-156-2   10.95

CLASS REUNION by Linda Hill. 176 pp. The girl from her past . . .
                                                   ISBN 1-56280-178-3   11.95

DREAM LOVER by Lyn Denison. 224 pp. A soft, sensuous, romantic fantasy. ISBN 1-56280-173-1 11.95

FORTY LOVE by Diana Simmonds. 288 pp. Joyous, heart-warming romance. ISBN 1-56280-171-6 11.95

IN THE MOOD by Robbi Sommers. 160 pp. The queen of erotic tension! ISBN 1-56280-172-4 11.95

SWIMMING CAT COVE by Lauren Douglas. 192 pp. 2nd Allison O'Neil Mystery. ISBN 1-56280-168-6 11.95

THE LOVING LESBIAN by Claire McNab and Sharon Gedan. 240 pp. Explore the experiences that make lesbian love unique. ISBN 1-56280-169-4 14.95

COURTED by Celia Cohen. 160 pp. Sparkling romantic encounter. ISBN 1-56280-166-X 11.95

SEASONS OF THE HEART by Jackie Calhoun. 240 pp. Romance through the years. ISBN 1-56280-167-8 11.95

K. C. BOMBER by Janet McClellan. 208 pp. 1st Tru North mystery. ISBN 1-56280-157-0 11.95

LAST RITES by Tracey Richardson. 192 pp. 1st Stevie Houston mystery. ISBN 1-56280-164-3 11.95

EMBRACE IN MOTION by Karin Kallmaker. 256 pp. A whirlwind love affair. ISBN 1-56280-165-1 11.95

HOT CHECK by Peggy J. Herring. 192 pp. Will workaholic Alice fall for guitarist Ricky? ISBN 1-56280-163-5 11.95

OLD TIES by Saxon Bennett. 176 pp. Can Cleo surrender to a passionate new love? ISBN 1-56280-159-7 11.95

LOVE ON THE LINE by Laura DeHart Young. 176 pp. Will Stef win Kay's heart? ISBN 1-56280-162-7 11.95

DEVIL'S LEG CROSSING by Kaye Davis. 192 pp. 1st Maris Middleton mystery. ISBN 1-56280-158-9 11.95

COSTA BRAVA by Marta Balletbo Coll. 144 pp. Read the book, see the movie! ISBN 1-56280-153-8 11.95

MEETING MAGDALENE & OTHER STORIES by Marilyn Freeman. 144 pp. Read the book, see the movie! ISBN 1-56280-170-8 11.95

SECOND FIDDLE by Kate Calloway. 208 pp. P.I. Cassidy James' second case. ISBN 1-56280-169-6 11.95

LAUREL by Isabel Miller. 128 pp. By the author of the beloved *Patience and Sarah*. ISBN 1-56280-146-5 10.95

LOVE OR MONEY by Jackie Calhoun. 240 pp. The romance of real life. ISBN 1-56280-147-3 10.95

SMOKE AND MIRRORS by Pat Welch. 224 pp. 5th Helen Black Mystery. ISBN 1-56280-143-0 10.95

DANCING IN THE DARK edited by Barbara Grier & Christine Cassidy. 272 pp. Erotic love stories by Naiad Press authors.
ISBN 1-56280-144-9   14.95

TIME AND TIME AGAIN by Catherine Ennis. 176 pp. Passionate love affair.
ISBN 1-56280-145-7   10.95

PAXTON COURT by Diane Salvatore. 256 pp. Erotic and wickedly funny contemporary tale about the business of learning to live together.
ISBN 1-56280-114-7   10.95

INNER CIRCLE by Claire McNab. 208 pp. 8th Carol Ashton Mystery.
ISBN 1-56280-135-X   11.95

LESBIAN SEX: AN ORAL HISTORY by Susan Johnson. 240 pp. Need we say more?
ISBN 1-56280-142-2   14.95

WILD THINGS by Karin Kallmaker. 240 pp. By the undisputed mistress of lesbian romance.
ISBN 1-56280-139-2   11.95

THE GIRL NEXT DOOR by Mindy Kaplan. 208 pp. Just what you'd expect.
ISBN 1-56280-140-6   11.95

NOW AND THEN by Penny Hayes. 240 pp. Romance on the westward journey.
ISBN 1-56280-121-X   11.95

HEART ON FIRE by Diana Simmonds. 176 pp. The romantic and erotic rival of *Curious Wine*.
ISBN 1-56280-152-X   11.95

DEATH AT LAVENDER BAY by Lauren Wright Douglas. 208 pp. 1st Allison O'Neil Mystery.
ISBN 1-56280-085-X   11.95

YES I SAID YES I WILL by Judith McDaniel. 272 pp. Hot romance by famous author.
ISBN 1-56280-138-4   11.95

FORBIDDEN FIRES by Margaret C. Anderson. Edited by Mathilda Hills. 176 pp. Famous author's "unpublished" Lesbian romance.
ISBN 1-56280-123-6   21.95

SIDE TRACKS by Teresa Stores. 160 pp. Gender-bending Lesbians on the road.
ISBN 1-56280-122-8   10.95

HOODED MURDER by Annette Van Dyke. 176 pp. 1st Jessie Batelle Mystery.
ISBN 1-56280-134-1   10.95

WILDWOOD FLOWERS by Julia Watts. 208 pp. Hilarious and heart-warming tale of true love.
ISBN 1-56280-127-9   10.95

NEVER SAY NEVER by Linda Hill. 224 pp. Rule #1: Never get involved with . . .
ISBN 1-56280-126-0   11.95

THE SEARCH by Melanie McAllester. 240 pp. Exciting top cop Tenny Mendoza case.
ISBN 1-56280-150-3   10.95

THE WISH LIST by Saxon Bennett. 192 pp. Romance through the years.
ISBN 1-56280-125-2   10.95

FIRST IMPRESSIONS by Kate Calloway. 208 pp. P.I. Cassidy James' first case.
ISBN 1-56280-133-3   10.95

SOMEONE TO WATCH by Jaye Maiman. 272 pp. 4th Robin
Miller Mystery. ISBN 1-56280-095-7 10.95

GREENER THAN GRASS by Jennifer Fulton. 208 pp. A young
woman — a stranger in her bed. ISBN 1-56280-092-2 10.95

TRAVELS WITH DIANA HUNTER by Regine Sands. Erotic
lesbian romp. Audio Book (2 cassettes) ISBN 1-56280-107-4 16.95

CABIN FEVER by Carol Schmidt. 256 pp. Sizzling suspense
and passion. ISBN 1-56280-089-1 10.95

THERE WILL BE NO GOODBYES by Laura DeHart Young. 192
pp. Romantic love, strength, and friendship. ISBN 1-56280-103-1 10.95

FAULTLINE by Sheila Ortiz Taylor. 144 pp. Joyous comic
lesbian novel. ISBN 1-56280-108-2 9.95

OPEN HOUSE by Pat Welch. 176 pp. 4th Helen Black Mystery.
ISBN 1-56280-102-3 10.95

FOREVER by Evelyn Kennedy. 224 pp. Passionate romance — love
overcoming all obstacles. ISBN 1-56280-094-9 10.95

WHISPERS by Kris Bruyer. 176 pp. Romantic ghost story
ISBN 1-56280-082-5 10.95

NIGHT SONGS by Penny Mickelbury. 224 pp. 2nd Gianna
Maglione Mystery. ISBN 1-56280-097-3 10.95

GETTING TO THE POINT by Teresa Stores. 256 pp. Classic
southern Lesbian novel. ISBN 1-56280-100-7 10.95

PAINTED MOON by Karin Kallmaker. 224 pp. Delicious
Kallmaker romance. ISBN 1-56280-075-2 11.95

THE MYSTERIOUS NAIAD edited by Katherine V. Forrest &
Barbara Grier. 320 pp. Love stories by Naiad Press authors.
ISBN 1-56280-074-4 14.95

DAUGHTERS OF A CORAL DAWN by Katherine V. Forrest.
240 pp. Tenth Anniversay Edition. ISBN 1-56280-104-X 11.95

BODY GUARD by Claire McNab. 208 pp. 6th Carol Ashton
Mystery. ISBN 1-56280-073-6 11.95

CACTUS LOVE by Lee Lynch. 192 pp. Stories by the beloved
storyteller. ISBN 1-56280-071-X 9.95

SECOND GUESS by Rose Beecham. 216 pp. 2nd Amanda
Valentine Mystery. ISBN 1-56280-069-8 9.95

A RAGE OF MAIDENS by Lauren Wright Douglas. 240 pp.
6th Caitlin Reece Mystery. ISBN 1-56280-068-X 10.95

TRIPLE EXPOSURE by Jackie Calhoun. 224 pp. Romantic
drama involving many characters. ISBN 1-56280-067-1 10.95

UP, UP AND AWAY by Catherine Ennis. 192 pp. Delightful
romance.   ISBN 1-56280-065-5   11.95

PERSONAL ADS by Robbi Sommers. 176 pp. Sizzling short
stories.   ISBN 1-56280-059-0   11.95

CROSSWORDS by Penny Sumner. 256 pp. 2nd Victoria Cross
Mystery.   ISBN 1-56280-064-7   9.95

SWEET CHERRY WINE by Carol Schmidt. 224 pp. A novel of
suspense.   ISBN 1-56280-063-9   9.95

CERTAIN SMILES by Dorothy Tell. 160 pp. Erotic short stories.
                                            ISBN 1-56280-066-3   9.95

EDITED OUT by Lisa Haddock. 224 pp. 1st Carmen Ramirez
Mystery.   ISBN 1-56280-077-9   9.95

WEDNESDAY NIGHTS by Camarin Grae. 288 pp. Sexy
adventure.   ISBN 1-56280-060-4   10.95

SMOKEY O by Celia Cohen. 176 pp. Relationships on the
playing field.   ISBN 1-56280-057-4   9.95

KATHLEEN O'DONALD by Penny Hayes. 256 pp. Rose and
Kathleen find each other and employment in 1909 NYC.
                                            ISBN 1-56280-070-1   9.95

STAYING HOME by Elisabeth Nonas. 256 pp. Molly and Alix
want a baby . . . or do they?   ISBN 1-56280-076-0   10.95

KEEPING SECRETS by Penny Mickelbury. 208 pp. 1st Gianna
Maglione Mystery.   ISBN 1-56280-052-3   9.95

THE ROMANTIC NAIAD edited by Katherine V. Forrest &
Barbara Grier. 336 pp. Love stories by Naiad Press authors.
                                            ISBN 1-56280-054-X   14.95

UNDER MY SKIN by Jaye Maiman. 336 pp. 3rd Robin Miller
Mystery.   ISBN 1-56280-049-3.   11.95

CAR POOL by Karin Kallmaker. 272pp. Lesbians on wheels
and then some!   ISBN 1-56280-048-5   10.95

NOT TELLING MOTHER: STORIES FROM A LIFE by Diane
Salvatore. 176 pp. Her 3rd novel.   ISBN 1-56280-044-2   9.95

GOBLIN MARKET by Lauren Wright Douglas. 240pp. 5th Caitlin
Reece Mystery.   ISBN 1-56280-047-7   10.95

LONG GOODBYES by Nikki Baker. 256 pp. 3rd Virginia Kelly
Mystery.   ISBN 1-56280-042-6   9.95

FRIENDS AND LOVERS by Jackie Calhoun. 224 pp. Mid-
western Lesbian lives and loves.   ISBN 1-56280-041-8   11.95

BEHIND CLOSED DOORS by Robbi Sommers. 192 pp. Hot,
erotic short stories.   ISBN 1-56280-039-6   11.95

CLAIRE OF THE MOON by Nicole Conn. 192 pp. See the
movie — read the book! ISBN 1-56280-038-8   10.95

THE SPY IN QUESTION by Amanda Kyle Williams. 256 pp.
4th Madison McGuire Mystery. ISBN 1-56280-037-X   9.95

SAVING GRACE by Jennifer Fulton. 240 pp. Adventure and
romantic entanglement. ISBN 1-56280-051-5   10.95

CURIOUS WINE by Katherine V. Forrest. 176 pp. Tenth Anniver-
sary Edition. The most popular contemporary Lesbian love story.
ISBN 1-56280-053-1   11.95
    Audio Book (2 cassettes) ISBN 1-56280-105-8   16.95

CHAUTAUQUA by Catherine Ennis. 192 pp. Exciting, romantic
adventure. ISBN 1-56280-032-9   9.95

A PROPER BURIAL by Pat Welch. 192 pp. 3rd Helen Black
Mystery. ISBN 1-56280-033-7   9.95

SILVERLAKE HEAT: A Novel of Suspense by Carol Schmidt.
240 pp. Rhonda is as hot as Laney's dreams. ISBN 1-56280-031-0   9.95

LOVE, ZENA BETH by Diane Salvatore. 224 pp. The most talked
about lesbian novel of the nineties! ISBN 1-56280-030-2   10.95

A DOORYARD FULL OF FLOWERS by Isabel Miller. 160 pp.
Stories incl. 2 sequels to *Patience and Sarah*. ISBN 1-56280-029-9   9.95

MURDER BY TRADITION by Katherine V. Forrest. 288 pp. 4th
Kate Delafield Mystery. ISBN 1-56280-002-7   11.95

THE EROTIC NAIAD edited by Katherine V. Forrest & Barbara
Grier. 224 pp. Love stories by Naiad Press authors.
ISBN 1-56280-026-4   14.95

DEAD CERTAIN by Claire McNab. 224 pp. 5th Carol Ashton
Mystery. ISBN 1-56280-027-2   9.95

CRAZY FOR LOVING by Jaye Maiman. 320 pp. 2nd Robin Miller
Mystery. ISBN 1-56280-025-6   10.95

STONEHURST by Barbara Johnson. 176 pp. Passionate regency
romance. ISBN 1-56280-024-8   9.95

INTRODUCING AMANDA VALENTINE by Rose Beecham.
256 pp. 1st Amanda Valentine Mystery. ISBN 1-56280-021-3   10.95

These are just a few of the many Naiad Press titles — we are the oldest and
largest lesbian/feminist publishing company in the world. We also offer an
enormous selection of lesbian video products. Please request a complete
catalog. We offer personal service; we encourage and welcome direct mail
orders from individuals who have limited access to bookstores carrying our
publications.